# The Possession of Blackstone Mansion

The Blackstone Trilogy Book 2
Augustine Pierce

Pierce Publishing

 Get your free book, *Zoe's Haunt*, by joining Augustine Pierce's newsletter. You can unsubscribe at any time.

Copyright © 2023 by Augustine Pierce

All rights reserved.

No portion of this book may be reproduced in any form without written permission from the publisher or author, except as permitted by U.S. copyright law.

# Contents

| | |
|---|---:|
| 1 | 1 |
| 2 | 9 |
| 3 | 19 |
| 4 | 31 |
| 5 | 44 |
| 6 | 63 |
| 7 | 70 |
| 8 | 80 |
| 9 | 98 |
| 10 | 105 |
| 11 | 118 |
| 12 | 128 |
| 13 | 146 |
| 14 | 159 |
| 15 | 176 |
| 16 | 193 |

| 17 | 205 |
| 18 | 219 |
| 19 | 224 |
| 20 | 230 |
| 21 | 245 |
| 22 | 266 |
| 23 | 276 |
| 24 | 291 |
| 25 | 302 |
| 26 | 315 |
| The Fall of Blackstone Mansion | 327 |
| Acknowledgments | 330 |
| Dark Realm | 331 |
| Also by Augustine Pierce | 332 |
| About the Author | 333 |

# 1

"Glad we finally got to do this." Katherine smiled as she held up her wineglass to clink with Kirk's. The candlelight made her deep, sea-blue eyes sparkle and cast a warm glow on her face, which contrasted nicely against her dark, wavy hair.

They were having a very exquisite dinner in a French restaurant in the downtown area of his town of Creek. She still lived a good twenty minutes away on the outskirts of the much smaller town of Blackstone, which had been named for the extremely wealthy family that founded it over a century and a half ago. As the duly appointed representative for the last living heir of the estate, part-time DJ and influencer Jordan Blackstone, she called his uninhabited mansion hidden in the foothills outside the town her current work site. She could have lived closer to it, but she wanted to be far enough from the town that she didn't run the danger of constantly bumping into its denizens, such as her former landlord.

"Almost thought it wouldn't happen," Kirk was tall and handsome, with his equally dark hair now growing out to a little past his eyes.

"I know, I know. I just..." She threw a glance at the windowsill, at its festive decorations of cotton-ball spiderwebs and Kleenex ghosts that foretold of the upcoming holiday, now only a little over two weeks away. *Kleenex. How quaint.*

She looked back at him and wondered if his lengthening hair was an attempt to make him even more attractive. If so, it was definitely working.

"Eileen's funeral, dealing with Jordan, I get it," Kirk said with a sympathetic smile.

He was referring not only to Katherine's current employer, but also her nearly solving the mystery behind the disappearance and death of Eileen Byrne more than a century ago at the hands of her fiancé, Reginald Blackstone, and his brother, Marcus.

Katherine had convinced Jordan to let her assess the value of and represent the estate in the sale of the antiques that had sat in the mansion ever since his ancestors had mysteriously abandoned it, seemingly out of nowhere, only a few short years after Eileen's death.

# THE POSSESSION OF BLACKSTONE MANSION

Katherine considered herself having only nearly solved Eileen's mystery because the cold, hard fact of the matter was that she would have gotten nowhere had it not been for the help of Eileen's ghost.

*I still can't believe it. Ghosts are real. And one of them reached out to me. Shared her memory of her last moments.* That experience had been the most intense, the most incredible, of Katherine's life. It was as if she'd been right there with Eileen, but she'd also experienced it as if she'd been watching a film, or more accurately, strapped into a VR headset.

She still hadn't given Kirk all the details. Not that she didn't trust him. He'd been unbelievably supportive of her, considering not only that tonight was their first official date, but they'd also only met a few weeks earlier. No, it was that she didn't fully believe it herself, and she was the one who had gone through it all.

"I mean, yeah, Jordan's a handful, but it's more the funeral." *Ghosts are real and I helped one, what, cross over?*

"What was it like? Seeing Eileen?" Kirk asked.

This was officially the first time he'd asked, but Katherine had known for weeks that he'd wanted to. She could just tell. He'd had an air of caution around her ever since the funeral and on more than one occasion, he'd looked like he'd wanted to ask her something, then either closed his mouth or actually said, "It's nothing."

"Cross over?" she asked.

"Is that what it's called?"

"I dunno. Antiques are my area of expertise, not any afterlife."

"You don't believe in it? Even after everything you've seen?"

"I've never really given it much thought."

"Not even after Dean's death?"

Dean, her lifelong best friend, who'd died in a car accident which she'd survived. From the time shortly after his funeral to only a few weeks ago, she'd developed this really weird habit of talking to him—as if he were right there on the other end of the phone—which she could only break once she'd admitted to Kirk how much she missed Dean.

She looked out the window.

"I'm sorry," Kirk said. "I didn't mean to sound so flippant."

"No, it's okay." She smiled at him, and sipped her tasty, but very marked-up, Maison Vieille, a cheap red table wine. She wasn't exactly an oenophile, but in her antiques career, she'd been inside enough wealthy clients' cellars to have a good sense of which bottles were highly sought after and which were not. "I just don't really know how to talk about any of this."

# THE POSSESSION OF BLACKSTONE MANSION

"Perfectly normal. I've heard ghost stories my whole life, but never met any myself and never met anyone who had."

"To answer your question, it was completely anti-climactic, Eileen's crossing."

"Really?"

"Yeah, I mean, she was there, next to this tree. She smiled at me, then she looked away, like someone had called her name."

"Loved ones who'd gone before her?"

"Maybe her and Vernon's baby?"

In the vision that Eileen had gifted Katherine, it had been revealed that the Blackstone patriarch, Vernon, had been carrying on an affair with Eileen around the time that she had been dating, and then become engaged to his son, Reginald. The affair, and her resulting pregnancy, was the indirect cause of her death as, upon learning of it, Reginald had flown into a rage and stabbed her, wounding her fatally, though not killing her immediately.

"Man, that is so messed up." Kirk shook his head.

Katherine nodded. "After she looks away and says whatever to whomever, she walks into the sunshine."

"So she just faded away?"

"Pretty much."

"No walking into a tunnel of light or anything?"

"I mean, maybe that's what *she* saw, but I just saw her kinda fade almost into a mist."

"Wow."

Katherine knew all of this was pretty insane to hear out loud, and she wished she could ease his sense of reality, but since she couldn't ease her own, she knew she'd be of little help to him and had decided since Eileen's funeral to simply answer any of his questions as honestly as she could. "Yeah."

"I'm sorry. We don't have to keep talking about this."

"It's fine. It's just a little uncomfortable, like we got off the world's most intense roller coaster."

"Odd way of putting it."

"When I come up with a better way, I'll update you."

"Can't wait. In the meantime, how are you finding your new place?"

Since her previous landlord, Drew, had weeks ago so unceremoniously booted her from his late father's tiny house, Kirk, Wendy, the ever-present server at Blackstone's only diner, and Jordan had all promised her recommendations. In the end, it had been Jordan's call. Katherine guessed it was the prestige that came with her association with someone of his so well-established Oregonian old money that had seized her current landlord's attention. That and it hadn't hurt that with her commission from having sold the first batch of Jordan's antiques, she'd been able to pay an entire six months' worth of rent

# THE POSSESSION OF BLACKSTONE MANSION

upfront. "It's great. Very roomy, comfortable. Huge TV, perfect Wi-Fi. Kitchen's got an island."

"You'll have to give me a tour."

"Why, Kirk Whitehead, are you inviting yourself over?"

"I mean, unless this first date is going horribly, which I don't think it is, that suggests there'll be a second."

"Aren't we just Captain Confidence?" *I shouldn't sleep with him on the first date. What am I, twenty-three? And I'm so much older. Might not be quite what he's used to.*

He smiled and tipped his glass toward her.

"Well, no, it's not going *horribly*, so if you play your cards right, you may be due a tour of the grand palace sooner than you think." She tipped her own glass.

Their desserts arrived, hers a chocolate *pot de crème* and his a crème brûlée. They chatted about lighter things, flirted, fed each other bites, and finally, it was time to go.

He drove them back to her place. On getting out, they hugged and dance-stumbled to the entrance to her modest, gray, six-story complex. There, they kept their embrace and faced each other. He smiled. She smiled wider.

*Yes, Kirk, kiss me now! Then I'm gonna take you up and we're gonna destroy that bed!*

## AUGUSTINE PIERCE

He leaned in. She stood on her tiptoes. He held her tighter. She wrapped her arms around his shoulders and neck. She squeezed. Her lips parted. He leaned in closer and closer. The night was about to become so perfect.

"Kat?" The male voice frightened her almost as much as her first encounter with Eileen's ghost.

## 2

"Did you hear—?" Kirk pulled out of his embrace with Katherine.

"I didn't hear anything." She practically had to hang from his shoulders to stay so close.

"Kat? Is that you?" the terribly familiar voice asked again.

Kirk and Katherine looked across the street at the same time. There stood a man almost as tall as Kirk, with dirty blond hair, rugged good looks, in a wool jacket and jeans. He leaned up against a black luxury sedan, his rental.

"Luke? What the hell are you doing here?" Katherine was hardly able to believe she saw her ex-boyfriend, Luke Callahan, directly in front of her.

Luke shrugged. "I had to see you."

Kirk stepped away from Katherine and offered Luke his hand. "Hi, I'm Kirk."

Luke accepted Kirk's gesture as if they'd been friends for years. "Like the captain."

# AUGUSTINE PIERCE

"The one and only."

*No, Kirk! Don't be* nice *to him!* She marched over to them, but kept her irritation focused squarely on Luke. "I'm sorry. I somehow missed the part where you explained what the hell you're doing here!"

"Just told you. Had to see you."

"Not good enough! First you call my mourning Dean 'whining,' then you flat-out dump me, then you, what, stick a tracking device on my jacket?"

"Wasn't that hard, Kat."

Kirk took a small step back. "You two clearly have a lot to unpack here."

"No, Kirk," Katherine said, "we don't because Luke was two seconds away from booting his ass as hard as he could back to New York."

"It's cool." Kirk leaned over and kissed Katherine's cheek. "I'll call you tomorrow."

*No, Kirk! I was gonna ride you so hard your head would've exploded!*

"Great to meet you, Kirk," Luke said in his nauseatingly charming way, and waved as Kirk got in his car.

Katherine also waved and held her hand in the telephone gesture to her cheek where Kirk had kissed her. She kept her eyes on his disappearing car. "You're such a dick."

"I didn't know you'd be on a date," Luke said.

"Go home, Luke." She walked back toward the entrance to her building.

"Kat, just two minutes. Please."

"Nope."

"One minute."

"It'll take us longer than that to get to my unit."

He caught up to her. "Kat, come on. I'm sorry."

She opened the door, but didn't hold it for him. "First time for everything." She walked to the elevator and poked the up button.

"I deserve that." He winced.

"And so, so much more." She got in the elevator, stabbed the fourth-floor button repeatedly, and made no effort to hold the elevator door open either.

He ran in and stood next to her.

"Seriously, Luke," she said. "You gotta go."

"One drink."

She scoffed at him. "Um, no." She faced forward.

"Half a drink."

"I know what you're trying to do. You think if you get some booze in me, flash those eyes, and beg enough, that I'll crumble, sleep with you, and forgive everything." She turned around long enough to catch him in the middle of a hopeful expression. She shook her head in disgust. "Such a prick."

## AUGUSTINE PIERCE

The elevator dinged. The door opened. She marched in a determined bee-line to her front door. She had no intention of granting him an inch.

"Yes, I know, I can be a prick, but come on, Kat, I flew all the way out here."

She didn't face him as she dug her keys out. *Why didn't I have these ready?* "How is that *my* problem?"

"It's not. I just want you to know how seriously I'm taking this—us."

She opened the door and finally faced him. "Fantastic, Luke. Why don't you call me two months ago, when I might've cared?" She went inside and started to close the door, but he jammed in his foot. "Okay, now you're getting creepy."

"Kat, please. I'm sorry."

"Already said that." She pushed the door a little against his foot, but he wasn't budging. She sighed, gave up, and turned inside. "Don't make me call the cops, Luke."

Her living room was quite spacious, with a burgundy sofa, ivory coffee table, and TV. A large set of windows provided a stunning view of the parking lot below. To the left was her dining room table and chairs, and her kitchen with its own little island. To the right was the narrow hallway to her bedroom and bathroom.

He eased the door open and closed it behind him. "Just one minute."

# THE POSSESSION OF BLACKSTONE MANSION

With a heavy sigh, she went to her fridge, taking out a chilled bottle of the finest Hacienda Antigua tequila. She set it on the counter next to the sink, in which soaked a frying pan crusted with the burnt remains of scrambled eggs. She took out a shot glass and poured one.

He frowned. "I see the drinking hasn't slowed."

She knocked back the shot and poured another. "How is that any of your goddamn business?"

He pursed his lips, clearly wanting to retort, but he didn't. He shifted awkwardly. Now that he'd forced his one minute, he didn't seem to know what to do with it.

"Well?" she asked.

"I was overwhelmed."

"Overwhelmed? Did *your* best friend die in a crash? Did *your* friends abandon you? Did *I* abandon you?"

"No. I didn't know how to support you and I freaked out. But, Kat, it was one fight."

"One fight?" she asked. His minimizing of the situation was so infuriating.

"We'd fought before, but then this time, you were just gone."

She poured herself a third shot, downed it, and slapped the glass on the counter. She sealed the bottle and put it back in the refrigerator. As she closed the door, she could already feel the effects of that smooth, distilled agave. It took her several more steps than she'd expected to make her way back to the counter.

Luke walked up behind her and put his hands on her sides to steady her.

"Don't *touch* me!" she shouted as she spun around to glare up at him.

"I'm sorry."

"Stop saying that!" she shouted even louder. She could feel the tears coming. She needed him out of here before they really started to roll. "Luke, you need to leave."

He held his palms up in surrender and slowly backed away toward the front door. "I'm going. I'll—"

She thrust her own interrupting palm up at him.

He finished in a near whisper. "Call you tomorrow."

She said nothing else as he sheepishly backed out the front door and closed it. *Wonder where he's staying. Probably somewhere in Portland. That mean he's gonna drive out every day, find me, and apologize again?* "God, I hope not," she groaned.

She wandered into the middle of her living room. She stared out the window onto the parking lot below. This was a solid apartment. She was glad to have it, glad that Jordan had vouched for her so that it was so easy to get, but she knew it would not work in the long run. Eventually, she'd need a view and better amenities. The fact was that having been a sought-after antiques dealer in New York for so many years had gotten her used to certain luxuries—easy access to public transportation, a seemingly infinite number of cuisines available twenty-four hours, luxury spa treatments—that she'd eventually want to have again here. And if not the same ones, the local Oregonian equivalents.

Having exhausted her fascination with the view of the parking lot, she retreated to the hallway. Without Kirk, she felt so alone. Even though they were just starting whatever they were starting, it felt so good to be with him. Even when they talked about uncomfortable things, she felt safe. Now that Luke had confronted her, all those awful old feelings surrounding Dean's death were boiling back up. The abandonment that she'd already thrown at Luke. The anger at so many friends who'd turned their backs on her. The sadness over never being able to talk to Dean again. The guilt that he'd been lost, but she'd survived. The frustration that their rescue hadn't arrived quickly enough. And that existential dread of what life meant, well, at all. *Will I ever be able to contact Dean? Could he contact me? I wonder how that'd work.*

And then came the tears. She hadn't even noticed them at first, but the wetness tickled her cheeks and she heard the drops quietly splatting on the floor.

She walked into the bathroom to splash her face, and was annoyed at seeing herself in the mirror. She'd forgotten to take off her jacket. She was reluctant to get it wet, but she was even more hesitant to expend time and energy to hike to the living room to take it off, then have to hike back.

She ran the water, pulled her hair back, cupped her hands, and filled them. *Ow, that's cold!* She dumped her cupped hands and opted to just wipe her face rather than splash. The gesture was distinctly less satisfying than she'd assumed it would be when she was standing in the living room.

She laughed at the frivolity of it all, at even the purpose of rinsing her face of tears when there was no one around to notice. She smiled at herself in the mirror. *Man, I sure could've used sleeping with Kirk. We probably would've been done by now, at least with our first go of it. Probably would've been lying all curled up in each other and chatting about whatever.*

With a little longing sigh, she wiped her hands.

There was a chill at the back of her neck. It was that now very familiar sensation she'd grown so accustomed to. The cold that told her that a spirit was nearby, probably even next to her. The feeling and its implications didn't frighten her anymore, but it still made her uncomfortable, and put her on her guard.

She was already looking in the mirror, so there was no need to turn around. She still studied the reflected background. No one was there.

She stepped away from the mirror, into the hallway. "Hello?" She knew this, too, was a futile gesture. What else she'd learned about the dead was if they didn't want to reveal themselves, they just didn't. She waited there another second, just in case someone—dead or alive—decided to leap out of the hallway closet.

Luke had been gone for minutes now. And no one else appeared. She returned to the living room, took off her jacket, and tossed it on the sofa.

That's when she noticed it. The left pane of her living room window was open about an inch. It was so little that she hadn't even heard any outside noises, but wide enough that it was letting in an icy breeze. *Was that the chill? I guess it could've traveled from here to the bathroom.* She walked over, closed the pane, and made sure it was sealed. *But did I leave it open when I left?* She scanned her living room, hallway, and kitchen. There was no sign of anyone. *I don't think I did, which means...* "Hello?"

There were only the muted sounds of outside, mostly cars driving by on the nearby highway.

"'Kay, I'm gonna get some chocolate mousse from the fridge, put on my jams, chill on the couch with a doc, then go to bed."

No one acknowledged her plan for the rest of the evening.

"Okay, I'm gonna do that now."

Still no response from the apartment.

With a quick nod at the space, she decided either she was alone or whoever else was there had decided not to bother her, and settled in for the evening.

# 3

Katherine was drifting in and out of lovely, lovely sleep when she heard her phone *buzz* and *buzz*. She reached for it, still used to the days, only weeks ago, when she'd been renting Drew's house's upper floor and kept passing out next to her phone and laptop.

Her fingers did not find her phone. She opened her eyes and saw that it was sitting on the nightstand. *Buzz buzz!* She scooted over to it, sat up a little, picked it up, and saw that it was Jordan calling. She wiped her eyes and answered. "Hey, Jordan."

"How's my favorite antiques dealer doing this lovely morning?"

"Favorite? I'm the only one you know."

"Oh, that Katherine Norrington wit!"

"What time is it?"

"Eight. Did I wake you up?"

"No. I mean, yes, technically, but no, I was getting up, anyway. What's up?"

"Nothing urgent. Wanted to see how we're doing."

"*I'm* doing fine."

"Great! Excellent. Glad to hear it. So, the house..."

"Um, yeah, so I need to go out there, check out the other pieces. Did you figure out the electricity?"

"Yeah, uh, it's gonna be a few days." His tone sounded like he hadn't even bothered reaching out to the electric company yet.

She didn't feel like calling him on his fib. "Okay, just the longer it takes, the longer my job's gonna take."

"I know. I'll call 'em Monday, I swear."

She rolled her eyes. *Whatever, Jordan.* "Anyway, I'll have to start moving pieces, which means I need to hire people."

"How many?" He sounded very nervous.

"Pieces or people?"

"Well, both, but let's start with people."

"I mean, depends on how quickly you want this process to go. If I only hire three, it'll take longer, and thus I'll have to retain them longer. If I hire twenty, it'll go a lot faster, but I'll have to hire twenty. And that's all assuming they're working under functioning lights."

"Monday. I'll call them Monday."

"Great."

"Maybe we can meet halfway on workers. How about ten?"

"We don't have to know that now. Also, I need to find storage space, preferably with some kind of showroom."

"Is there anything like that all the way out there in Boonietown?"

"To be honest, I haven't done much looking, but yeah, I kinda doubt it."

"So, what are you gonna do?"

"I'll find something. I just don't know that it'll be right down the street."

"And I'm paying for that space too, right?"

"You can present your pieces however you'd like. If I do it, I'll have to cut corners."

"No, no, that's fine. Send my people the invoice."

"Will do."

"So, what's the timeline on all this space finding and people hiring?"

"I was planning on looking for a store Monday, also starting the conversation with potential workers."

"Good. Okay, good. And then...?"

"Hard to say. Unless I find space nearby that has a lot of, well, space, I'll have to do the house in sections, maybe even rooms. It's probably gonna be weeks to clear everything out."

"Weeks?"

"Again, Jordan, it all depends on how many workers, et cetera. You don't have to worry. I'll get through the pieces as quickly as possible and find the best buyers. I'm gonna make you a fortune."

The sound of his voice told her he was smiling. "I like the sound of that," he said.

"I thought you would." She scooted out of bed and stretched. "All right, I'm gonna go. I'll text or call if there are any updates. You call the electric company."

"I'll call them. I swear. I'll call them."

"When?"

"I'll call them, Kat."

"Well, hurry."

"I'll call."

"I'd appreciate that."

"Okay, Kat. Thanks so much."

"Thank you. Talk to you soon." She hung up and sighed. "Rich people."

She got showered and dressed. As she passed through the living room, she stared at the left window pane, which the previous night had been open.

It was still closed. *So did I open it last night and forgot? That doesn't make sense. Winter's right around the corner.* She glared suspiciously at the pane as if it, or the entire window, were about to jump off its frame and dance.

The window and its pane remained still.

She started fixing herself a smoothie. As she blended the ingredients, her eyes fell onto the still-soaking frying pan. "Oh right." She dumped it and inspected the burnt-egg residue. "That's why I opened the window!" She felt so relieved. *God, I'm getting paranoid!* Then again, after what she'd seen and experienced, of course she would be.

She finished blending her smoothie, downed it, and marched to the door. As she reached for the knob, she stopped and turned around. *That pane.* She gazed at it, doubts still lingering. Her eyes darted between the frying pan and the windows. Satisfied that she had, in fact, opened the latter due to the former, she got on with her day.

---

*I should call Kirk*, Katherine thought as she drove in to Blackstone. *No, he said he was gonna call me. I should wait for him to call me.* She reached the town square, which was looking particularly green and picturesque under the cool morning sun. *No, I should call him. Make sure he understands Luke and I are done.* Distracted, she turned off the square's west side and drove down three blocks. *Make sure it doesn't get awkward between us. Again.* She thought she remembered a storefront when she'd first moved here that had seemed like a decent place to set up shop. *Or maybe I should give him a day. Or two. I dunno.* She didn't remember exactly where the storefront was, drove north three blocks, didn't see it, turned around, and drove south five blocks. She saw it.

It had a dirty, cream-colored wall, enormous windows, and a slanted red awning that reminded her of the Pizza Huts from her childhood. A huge sad, blue sign hung in the window that said For Rent and gave a number.

She parked right in front, got out, and walked up to the sign. Inside, the space was almost entirely empty, but for a paint can in the back right corner, which she guessed had been abandoned by workers who'd cleared out the previous tenant's furniture. She also saw what looked like some office space in the back. "This could work. Put all the stuff in front, me in back, hire a part-timer for when I'm at the mansion or wherever." *No, I should call him.*

She called the number on the sign. It picked up immediately. An outgoing message played the voice of a middle-aged man. "You've reached Cameron and Associates. We're not here to take your call. Please call back during normal business hours and we'll happily attend to all your real-estate needs."

"Hi, this is Katherine Norrington. I'm calling regarding the property on west Third in Blackstone." She left her number, thanked them, hung up, and exhaled. *One thing down.*

# THE POSSESSION OF BLACKSTONE MANSION

She got into her car and drove the few blocks to Blackstone's diner, where her friendly acquaintance Wendy seemed to always be working.

The front door's bells jingled. Katherine found the sound very comforting. It was a reminder of the town's brighter side, not her former landlord Drew nor the creepy mansion on the hill that had already freaked her out more than once, but rather the pleasantness of Wendy's caring demeanor and the diner's comforting view of the town square.

Katherine found a seat before Wendy noticed she was there. She regarded the three-piece collections of paper pumpkin decorations that dotted the corners of the counter. *Halloween. So fun when you're a kid. Now a friggin' reality show.* She picked up a menu even though she already knew what she was going to get. It was what she almost always got. Hot cocoa with a side of omelet. This time, she'd be adventurous and make it a Greek one.

"'Morning, Kat. What can we get you?" Wendy asked.

"Hey, Wendy. 'Morning. The usual, but this time a Greek omelet."

"Oh, celebrating something, are we?"

"Ha-ha. Nah, just wanna mix it up. Actually, I think I'm gonna rent that space on Third."

"Oh, the, uh..." Wendy snapped her fingers in the air trying to remember the place in question.

# AUGUSTINE PIERCE

Katherine nodded. "Cream and red. Yeah."

"What're you gonna do with it?"

"Sell the stuff I drag outta the mansion."

Wendy leaned in and spoke in a low, concerned tone. "Hon, I don't think folks 'round here can afford what the Blackstones kept locked away out there."

"No, no, only to keep it and show off to the prospective buyers I'll be contacting."

"Oh! I was gonna say. Good luck pawning off antique sofas to these boys." She pointed a thumb behind her at the usual gaggle of men in trucker caps parked along the counter.

"Honestly, in some ways, that might be easier. Fewer people to track down."

Wendy nodded like she was following, but her blank expression said otherwise. "I'll get that in for ya," she said, referring to Katherine's order.

Katherine took out her phone. *I really should call Kirk. At least text him.* But she didn't text him. She texted Jordan instead.

# THE POSSESSION OF BLACKSTONE MANSION

> You sure about that?

> We're not opening it to Portland hipsters. I just need a place to keep and show off the pieces. Our prospectives will be happy to come out here for them.

> They'd be happier to take a 10-min taxi from pdx

> It'd cost more to rent a space in Portland and move all the stuff up there. And more time.

> So you've started the rental process?

> Yeah. Reached out to the owner. Hopefully, hear back Monday.

> Keep me updated

> Of course.

She set her phone on the counter. She stared at it. *You texted Jordan. Now text Kirk.* "I don't even know what to say," she told the device.

"What's that, hon?" Wendy served Katherine her food.

"Nothing. Thinkin' out loud."

"Well, let me know if you need anything else."

"Thanks, Wendy. Just the bill."

"Comin' right up."

## AUGUSTINE PIERCE

Katherine picked up her phone and fiddled with it. *Gotta eat.* She put it in her pocket and ate her breakfast.

Outside, she was still debating on whether to text Kirk. *I dunno what to say. "Sorry my ex showed up out of literal nowhere and totally ruined our night"? I should ask him out. A make-up dinner.* As she contemplated her options, she felt a *buzz* in her pocket. She took out her phone and checked the ID. Luke. She unlocked her phone and tapped on the text.

> Kat, please, I'm begging you. Just meet me. Please.

A thought crept up. *Maybe he deserves a second—*"No." She stopped in her tracks. "He wasn't there for me. At all. He practically made fun of my mourning over Dean."

She got in her car, closed the door, but didn't put on her seat belt. *I gotta talk to Kirk. Even if we don't go on another date, he's the only one I know with contacts who can move stuff out of the mansion. I can look elsewhere, but that means looking elsewhere!* She heaved a deep sigh and started typing a text.

> Hey K, really sorry about last night. You don't have to worry, though. Not with Luke. Gonna make sure he doesn't bother me again. Really wanna see you.

# THE POSSESSION OF BLACKSTONE MANSION

She paused before tapping send, then erased the message. She placed her phone on the dashboard mount and stared at it. Finally strapping in, she fired up the engine and drove home.

Entering her apartment, she dumped her purse on the sofa. She took off her jacket, tossed it too, and went to her bedroom. She opened her laptop and started a documentary on the history of the Caribbean island of Hispaniola. As the opening credits ran, her phone *buzzed*. She picked it up. It was Kirk. She lifted her finger to tap answer, but paused. She waited for it to stop *buzzing*. The notification soon popped up, telling her she had a message. She stared at the notification until it disappeared and set her phone down. She kept her eyes on it. *Just listen to it. No, he's gonna dump me. Technically, you're not really together, so he can't dump you.* "I'm such a coward," she told the phone. She continued her documentary.

Two hours later, with the documentary finished, but lacking anything else to do or the courage to even listen to Kirk's message, she cleaned up the dishes and continued with more documentaries till night-time. She passed out, still feeling nervous and guilty over Kirk.

The next day, she slept in. When she got up, she checked her phone to see if Kirk had called again. He had not. She got up, took a shower, and got dressed. She headed out and took a twenty-minute walk around the neighborhood. *Call him back without listening to the message. You can totally say you didn't even notice it.* "I'll visit tomorrow. First thing. Do it in person."

Somewhat satisfied with her decision, she returned home and repeated the same routine as the day before, this time with documentaries on the history of Halloween.

About a third of the way through the second documentary, her phone *buzzed*. It was Luke calling. She silenced her phone and set it aside. She continued watching in peace.

**4**

The next morning, Katherine woke up bright and early. The idea of driving out to Creek to meet Kirk as he arrived to work terrified her, so she decided to make some breakfast and figure it out from there.

As she was scrambling her eggs, her phone vibrated on the kitchen's island. She scooped it up and saw that it was Jordan calling. *At least he didn't wake me up this time.* She answered. "Hey, Jordan. Good morning."

"Did I wake you again?"

"Nope."

"What are your plans for today?"

"Actually—"

"Great. I need you to get out to the mansion in an hour."

"Why?"

"I finally called the electric company. They need to size the place up since they have no record of it."

"No record?"

"Nope."

"That's weird."

"Yeah. They're not even sure if they can wire it since it's so old. God, this is gonna cost me!"

"Sorry, I missed the part about why I need to go out there." She didn't have an enormous problem going, but she also didn't love the idea of hovering while some guy tested wires.

"They need someone to let them on to the property."

"Why can't you do that? You're the owner."

Jordan laughed with an edge of sarcasm. "Yeah, drive all the way out to Boonieville just to hang around while some guy pokes and prods at wires?"

*He thinks he owns me. And he's right.* "All right. I'll get going." *Kirk'll have to wait.* She had to admit she felt relieved. Then again, the more she put off talking to him, the more she dreaded it.

"Great. If you can be out there by 9:30. Any questions he has you can't answer, just pass them along."

*At which point you'll ignore them for a week.* "Okay. I'll finish up here and get going."

"You're the best."

"Don't I know it." She hung up, finished her breakfast, and set out for the mansion. On her way, she figured she'd follow up on that potential store. She rang Cameron and Associates.

# THE POSSESSION OF BLACKSTONE MANSION

"Cameron and Associates," answered a young male voice. "How may I direct your call?"

"Hi, this is Katherine Norrington. I left a message over the weekend."

"Message, right..." He sounded like he was looking it up.

"I was calling to find out if the property on west Third in Blackstone is still available."

"Blackstone..."

"It's cream with the red roof?"

"Oh, you're way out in, like, right next to Mt. Hood!"

"Yeah."

"Looks like it's available, yes. How soon did you want to move in?"

"Immediately."

"Great. Name of your business, Ms. Norrington?"

*Oh, right. That.* As usual, as Dean had always teased her, she had zero plan. "Uh, just put down Norrington Antiques."

"Selling antiques in Blackstone?"

"Yes, but not to Blackstone-ians."

The man scoffed. "Right? I bet. And where can we reach you?"

*I left you a message! Just check that!* She gave him her number and e-mail address.

"Great. I'll pass your information on to Mr. Cameron. You should hear from him soon."

# AUGUSTINE PIERCE

"Wonderful. Thanks so much."

"Have a nice day, Ms. Norrington."

"You too." She hung up.

---

Katherine arrived at the mansion's gate and parked in her usual spot to the right of the gate's doors.

No one else was there.

*Am I early?* She checked the time. Nine thirty. *Nope. Right on time.* She sat in her car for five minutes. Nobody showed. She got out, shivered at that minus-ten-degree difference between here and in town. She paced up and down the road for another five minutes. Still, no one showed. Sick of the cold, she got back in her car. She took her phone off its mount, fired up *Fruit Ninja*, and played a few rounds. She checked the time. Ten. *Where is this guy?*

She got out of the car and peered down the road, hoping that she'd see a van approaching from the distance.

Nothing.

"Okay." She got back in the car, and promised herself she'd only wait another five before calling Jordan. That's when her phone *buzzed*. It was him. She picked up, ready to chew him out.

He spoke immediately. "Kat!"

# THE POSSESSION OF BLACKSTONE MANSION

"Um..."

"Don't hate me."

"What's goin' on? I've been here almost forty minutes."

"Please don't hate me."

"What? He's not coming?"

"I kinda got the date wrong."

"What? Jordan, I've got things to do!"

"I know, I know. Don't hate me. I just... In my haste to get the electric company's visit set up, I screwed up the date."

"So, when are they coming?"

He sounded like he was wincing. "Next week."

She rolled her eyes hard. "Great."

"I know. I'm sorry."

She repeated herself. "I've got things to..."

"Promise it won't happen again."

"It's fine. Whatever. I'll just..." She sighed. "I'll call you."

"Okay. Sorry. Bye." He hung up.

*Goddamn it, Jordan! I'm not your errand girl! I mean, I am, but come on!* She got out of her car and slammed the door. *Well, I'm here. Might as well, I dunno, look at another room or two.* "Crap. Guess Kirk'll have to wait."

She marched through the gate and straight up the hill. At the mansion's front doors, she took out her flashlight. She realized that, unlike in previous weeks when she'd experienced gut-wrenching dread every time she approached the house, this time she felt nothing. *Is it 'cause I'm pissed off at Jordan or 'cause I know Eileen's moved on, so everything's done?* She knew everything was not finished with this fortress of a home. Not even close.

She went inside, turned on her flashlight, and headed to the door to the right of the staircase, the one she'd initially gone through on her first visit. She walked to the second door in the short hallway. *The music room.*

She opened the door and shone her flashlight all around. Sofas, chairs, tables, and that gorgeous harpsichord. *Yeah, let's do this one next.*

Satisfied, she backed out into the hallway. She was about to get on with the rest of her day when she had the instinct to peer to her right, past the west-east hallway, where if she continued, she'd end up at the north tower.

She walked along till she entered a corridor with the same dimensions as the west-east one. *Think this'll take me to the north tower.* She wasn't sure why that direction drew her so strongly, but she had the impulse to go there, ignoring the many doors she was passing along the way. *Since it's directly below the master, who knows? Maybe it has some interesting stuff.*

She arrived at the north tower. Like its upstairs equivalent, it had a set of huge double doors. Unlike the master's, though, these weren't decorated with any flourishes or a giant B. In fact, considering the style of the rest of the mansion, from its colors to its sculptures to its furniture, these doors were greatly understated.

Gripping the right doorknob, she twisted it, and pushed it forward. She wasn't sure why she was restraining herself so much. She'd already practically busted into the master bedroom upstairs. Maybe it was her not knowing what lay inside. She didn't want to fling the door open and knock its edge into some priceless metal floor globe.

Stepping inside, her flashlight revealed a semicircular library space. Like much of the rest of the mansion she'd seen, it contained the usual cobweb-covered sofas and chairs placed in the center of the room. Unlike the other library in the house's front, though, it boasted neither the size of bookshelves nor number of volumes. It looked more like one man's private area. *Vernon's mindfulness room? The obscenely wealthy nineteen-twenties equivalent?*

She let her light drift across the furniture and bookshelves. She spotted no piece that piqued her interest. Then a thought occurred to her. *Why's it semicircular? It's only half the area of the master upstairs!* The idea of what that insinuated excited her. She scanned the flat wall of bookshelves in front of her for any obvious opening into another room.

She found nothing.

Undeterred, she approached the bookshelves and scrutinized them. She swept her light across the book spines. She looked up and down the bookshelves' edges.

A metallic gleam.

She spotted it near the floor. Stooping for a closer look, she saw it was a hinge, likely steel. "All right." She stood up and stepped back to orient herself among the shelves. The hinge was attached to the lower-right corner of the shelf farthest to the left, where the flat wall met the semicircular one.

There, at the left-hand edge at about shoulder height, she located a steel lever. "Pretty obvious for a hidden room." She pulled it. With an uneasy, grinding squeak, the bookshelf slid out toward her and then to the right. It looked like a monster's jaw opening wide to devour her whole down its black, cave-like throat.

She stepped in to find the most ancient-looking room she'd so far seen in the mansion. It resembled the secret lair of a mad scientist straight out of a Wells or Lovecraft novel. A quick 180 revealed dense cobwebs stretched among overly packed bookcases against the semicircular left wall and a small, simple wooden desk and chair against the flat right wall. Upon the desk lay various scattered papers, a long-since dried inkwell, and a handsome black dip pen emblazoned with a gold B. "Damn, Blackstone. That's a Mason dip. You blew cash on everything."

She pressed forward, wiping cobwebs out of her way. She turned left to get a better look at those bookcases. The first one that caught her eye contained very worn leather-bound tomes such as *Sons of Elam: A History of Persia*, *Riches of the Black Land*, and *The Rise and Fall of the Xia Dynasty*. "Huh. The semi-legendary Chinese ruler. Wouldn't have pegged you folks as sinophiles."

She turned to face the desk, where her flashlight's beam located something that made her adrenaline surge. The unadorned door of a small square iron safe. It had two large keyholes on top of each other near its left edge. "Hello. What do we have here?" She stood right next to the desk for a closer look. "Must've kept those keys pretty nearby." She slid out the desk's main drawer.

No keys.

"Hm," she said out loud to the rest of the room. "Where could they be?" She guessed that wherever they were, it was some place fairly obvious as given the little she knew of the Blackstone men, none of them was fond of hard work, so wouldn't have made the keys' location a challenge to find. They probably wanted them out of plain sight, out of the reach of children and wives.

She looked over the bookcases with her flashlight. She saw no small boxes or other likely key containers. For just a second, she pointed the light out the room's opening, but that didn't feel right. *Those keys must be in this study.*

She faced the bookcases again. *I wonder.* She walked back to the desk, pulled out its chair, and sat. She scooted the chair around so that her light pointed in a straight line perpendicular with the front edge of the desk. *Black Land* lay at the dead center of the beam.

"Is it that obvious? *Riches of the Black Land?*" she asked the book. She stood and walked over to it. She attempted to take it out of the case, but found it had been wedged in tightly. She worked its spine up and down, trying to loosen it. After a few seconds, she'd freed an inch. Getting a better grip, she pulled a little harder. Finally, it slid out.

She held it flat in her palms. She opened the cover and thumbed past the first few pages. Reaching the table of contents, she thought she saw the slightest dip down the middle of the page. Turning it, she indeed found a hollowed-out section in which lay two large, bulky keys. She smiled as she set the book on the desk. "Boo-ya!"

She removed the keys and held them up. "I mean, Jordan gave me the run of the place." She grew even more excited. Whatever was behind that safe door was likely the most treasured item of the entire house.

She set her flashlight on the desk, pointed up. She held the two keys in front of the safe. It was a fifty-fifty chance which one went where. She inserted the key in her left hand into the upper hole, the other one in the lower. She tried to turn the upper one. It didn't budge. She grunted and switched keys. The top one turned to the right, the bottom to the left.

*Thunk!* The door opened a crack. She eased it the rest of the way, but saw nothing inside. She picked up her flashlight and pointed it at the open cavity. Inside, she found a black satin bag. She reached in and attempted to pick it up. It was very heavy. "Whoa." She had to lift it out with both hands. She set it on the desk, away from the pen and papers. She peeled back the sack.

Black and platinum. It was an ornament. She gripped it between her fingertips and lifted it out of the sack. She held it over her flashlight.

It was a palm-sized pendant with a dangling silver chain. Composed of five bars, the pendant was fashioned from a black metal she didn't recognize, arranged into a strange, esoteric symbol. A simple equilateral triangle was the major component, with little circles affixed at each corner. The last two bars stretched from the central points of two of the triangle's bars, passed through its center, and connected past its third bar in a V-shape, with a little circle at the end. A narrow, platinum vein ran down the center of each of the bars.

"What the hell is this?" The pendant's symbol looked familiar, but she had no idea why. "Looks like it's platinum with... What kind of metal is that?"

She noticed that as brightly as the embedded vein shone in the flashlight's beam, the surrounding black reflected nothing at all. It was as if the metal devoured the light's photons the moment they struck it.

She felt intense curiosity about the piece. Judging by where she'd found it, she guessed that not only did Jordan not know of its existence, but that it pointed to something deep in the family's history. She wondered why such a strange piece was locked away in this private study.

Feeling like a kid swiping a pack of Starburst from a convenience store, she put the pendant back in the bag and slid it into her purse.

She had the instinct to leave. Immediately. She grabbed her flashlight and left the room, sliding the bookshelf closed behind her. She hurried down the hallways and out of the mansion.

Once outside, she felt somewhat safe. She looked back at the house as if she might witness another ghost's appearance as she had with Eileen's.

# THE POSSESSION OF BLACKSTONE MANSION

She saw nothing, no one. "No chill either." She reflected on the whole time she'd spent in the mansion today. She hadn't seen nor felt any inkling of any spirits. "Was Eileen the only one, after all?"

She gave the mansion's tower attic windows one last glance, saw no one, and headed down the hill.

# 5

Katherine was halfway back to Blackstone when her phone *buzzed*. She answered it.

"Ms. Norrington?" an unfamiliar male voice asked over the car speakers.

"Speaking?"

"It's Dan Cameron of Cameron and Associates."

*Cameron and Associates...*

"You'd expressed interest in renting the unit on Third in Blackstone?"

"Oh right! Of course. Yes, Dan. Thanks for calling me back so quickly."

"Not a problem."

"Yeah, my associate, Jordan Blackstone, is interested in renting the space for me."

"Jordan Blackstone?"

"That's right."

"He named after the town?" Dan sounded very baffled.

"No, the, uh, town's named after his family."

# THE POSSESSION OF BLACKSTONE MANSION

"Huh." Dan was silent for a second, probably considering those implications. "Well, if Mr. Blackstone is the one actually renting, I'll, of course, have to speak with him."

"I understand. I can forward your information."

"And how are you involved in all this?"

"Jordan's renting the place for me so that I can use it as storage and a showroom for the antiques I move from his family's mansion east of Blackstone."

"Antiques, huh?"

"Yep."

"How long did you and Mr. Blackstone plan on staying at the property?"

"I mean, if I'm any good at my job, not longer than, say, three months. There are a few variables involved, but the goal is to sell his items, and that's it."

"So Norrington Antiques will exist solely for this one estate sale?"

"Not sure about the long term, but for now, yeah."

"Huh." He sounded even more doubtful and was silent for another long second. "Minimal lease is usually for two to five years."

"Yeah?"

"But you're only planning on staying for three months?"

*Great. Shouldn't have been so specific.* "Could be longer." She knew she was now encroaching in on lying territory. The fact was, if everything worked out, the time spent at the property in question would be a month max.

"I don't know, Ms. Norrington. That's an awfully small account."

While she thought she could find something else, she didn't want to deal with that, so went for broke. "Let me ask you something, Dan."

"What's that?"

"How long has this property been on the market?"

He hesitated between each word. "It's been a minute."

"And in the last month, how many calls for it?"

He was now so quiet, she for a second thought the call had dropped. "A few," he finally said.

She grinned, knowing that she had him in the corner. "Dan. How many?"

"I admit it's been quiet."

"Why don't we do this? I'll convince Jordan to rent for six months. During that time, you work on him to extend to a full year."

"If you only need it for one month, how are you gonna convince him to rent for six, let alone for a year?"

"You're in the sales business, aren't you?"

"Yeah."

"So sell him."

# THE POSSESSION OF BLACKSTONE MANSION

"What is it you get out of this little conspiracy, Ms. Norrington?"

"Storage and showroom I don't have to pay for, a nice cushion of time, close access to the mansion, and best of all?"

"Yeah?"

"I can stop looking."

"That makes sense."

"So I'll text you Jordan's information. I'll send him yours. He'll hopefully get on the horn soon, then you can let me know when the deal's done."

"Won't you be hearing from him?"

*You'd think so, yes.* She didn't want to tell him that Jordan could be a huge flake. She put on a big smile. "I guess whoever gets to me first!"

"Sounds good, Ms. Norrington. I'll eagerly await your text."

"You have a good one, Dan." She hung up. She then dictated a text to Jordan.

> Think I may have found our place.

*Now to Kirk.*

She drove through Blackstone and got on the highway. She was already feeling her adrenaline surge all over again after having ignored Kirk all weekend. It was only twenty minutes to his office in Creek. She jumped out of her car, waltzed in, and confronted the scowl of his coworker, Annie.

"Good morning, Ms. Norrington," Annie sneered. "How can I help you?"

"Is he in back?" Katherine asked.

"Maybe." Annie leaned back in her chair with evil-Bond-villain cockiness.

"I could just call to him."

"And I could just have you arrested."

"On what charge?"

"Oh I dunno. Trespassing."

"I'm a potential customer."

"Harassment."

"Please. You haven't seen my 'harassment.'"

"I have a feeling anything'd work. I've heard all about your run-ins with the law."

"What do you mean you've heard?"

Annie grinned.

"He told you, didn't he?" Katherine asked.

Annie shrugged as if to say "I don't know." "To be fair, I kinda dragged it outta him. He seems to really like you," she said in a tone that also said "And I have no idea why."

Katherine leaned in and spoke in a harshly quiet tone. "Look, Annie, I get that you're madly in love with Kirk—"

Annie scoffed, but it didn't sound convincing at all. "Um, I have a boyfriend."

# THE POSSESSION OF BLACKSTONE MANSION

"Yeah, we've all had"—Katherine held up air quotes—"'boyfriends' when we were really mad for the boy next door who didn't know we existed."

"He knows I exist!" Annie nearly shouted.

"Who knows who exists?" Kirk entered, tapping out a syncopated rhythm on the folder he was holding.

*Always drumming. Wonder if he'll ever let me hear him play for reals.*

"Nothing. Nobody." Annie buried her face in her monitor.

"Oh, hey, Kat," Kirk said. "Didn't hear from you."

"Yeah, I figured I'd just drop by," Katherine said.

"Oh, well, uh, I'm kinda at work."

"I know." Katherine looked down at Annie. "Can I borrow him for, like, two minutes?"

Annie didn't lift her eyes off her monitor. "Gonna bring him back?"

Katherine took that as permission and gave Kirk the biggest pleading puppy-dog eyes she could muster. "Pwetty pwease?"

Kirk cracked a grin. "Annie, you gonna be okay?"

Annie still didn't remove her gaze from her monitor. "I'll manage." She spun around in her chair. "Somehow."

"Thanks. You're the best." Kirk pointed to the door and headed out. "Two minutes." he told Katherine.

As he stepped outside, he gave her a sad grin. "You ghosted me."

"No, Kirk, I really didn't. I—" *Come on, Kat. You did.*

"So, look, Kat, it's fine. You and Luke. We had one dinner. I'm a big boy."

"No, Kirk, I am *not* with Luke. I left him."

"He doesn't seem to think so."

"Well, that's his problem. I left, I'm here, and I'd like to see you again. Like, 'see you' see you."

"How you gonna get rid of him?"

"I was thinking ax to the back of the head, dismemberment, then a shallow grave out in the woods."

He laughed, but also sounded a little taken aback. "Awfully specific."

"It's true that Luke and I were close-ish once. But with Dean's death, it all unraveled quickly. I guess I'm still angry about it."

"That it ended?"

"No! That Luke was such a dick."

"So for real, how you gonna clue him in?"

She sighed. "I will probably have to talk to him at some point, yes, but honestly, that's so far outta my mind right now. I'm just trying to get everything set up with the mansion."

"Oh, right. How's that going?"

"Well, funny you should ask. Jordan's authorized me to hire ten guys to help out. Moving a room at a time. As fast as we can."

"Ten? Really?"

"Yes, and it'll be for several days' work."

"Oh."

"So, do you know nine guys you can recommend?"

"I think I could scrape some up."

"Wonderful. Well, you go scraping and we can talk about it more over hot dogs and beer at bowling."

"Bowling?"

"Yes. I want to take you, Kirk Whitehead, on a date out bowling."

"Hate to admit it, but I'm a terrible bowler."

"Perfect. So am I. We can be terrible together."

He nodded slowly and grinned wide. It looked like she was finally winning him over.

"Unless, uh, you think Annie would have a problem with that," Katherine said.

"Annie? What's she got to do with it?"

*Oh crap! He doesn't know! Of course he doesn't know!* "Nothing. Just figured there might've been some intra-office romance at some point."

He shook his head in complete bafflement. "No. She's just a friend."

*Oh, how little you know.* "All right, then. Now I've just gotta find an alley."

## AUGUSTINE PIERCE

"There's a place in Oregon City. Bit of a drive, but the dogs are good and bottomless drinks."

"I love drives. And bottomless drinks."

"Then King's Lanes it is."

"Sounds like you've been there before."

"Once or twice."

"Ah, I get it. Where you take all the girls."

He grinned and blushed. "Once or twice."

"I'll pick you up, say, 7:00 Friday?"

"Sounds great."

She opened her arms for a hug. He embraced, but she could feel resistance. As much as she'd reassured him, he was probably still stuck on Luke. *Goddamn it, Luke. Why'd you have to show up?* When she and Kirk pulled away from their hug, she reiterated, "And we'll chat all about the new gig."

"That we will." He headed back in.

"Have a wonderful week, Kirk. I'll text you."

"You too, Kat." He disappeared inside.

*I hope Annie notices that spring in his step.* Katherine got in her car, closed the door, dug out her phone, and texted Jordan.

> Think I may have found our guys.

She fired up the engine and got on the road. Her phone *buzzed* as she was nearing Blackstone. It was Jordan. She answered. "Hey, Jordan."

"I've been speaking with a Dan Cameron."

"Yeah, the landlord of the place I want us to rent."
"Me to rent."
"Right."
"For a year."

*Great, Dan. I told you to pitch that after I'd had my chance.* "Uh-huh?"

"I thought you only needed the place a month."

"I honestly don't know, Jordan. A month, six, it depends on a lot of things, not the least of which is getting your items outta the mansion."

"You told me that'd take days."

"I think I said it *could* take days, but that's on the bare minimum."

"So let me get this straight. You're asking me to rent commercial real estate in Blackstone, Oregon, for at least six months for items that you hope to sell in less than a month? Is that about right?"

"I think six months would be a good"—she couldn't think of any better word, so went with what she'd told Dan—"cushion."

"Funny. That's what Mr. Cameron said."

*Great. Now it sounds like we're conspiring to fleece Jordan for something I don't even really need.* "I would prefer not being bound by the month-long deadline."

"I never said it was a deadline."

"I understand that, but... Can we just-can we go for six months and call it good?"

He sighed, which she'd learned was his version of "okay." "There's also the matter of the insurance."

"All right?"

"The cheapest I could find was with a local firm."

*Oh no. Please, no.* "Oh?"

"It's called Blackstone Insurance. Those Blackstone-ites sure don't skimp on creativity."

"Guess not."

"There's a problem, though."

"What's that?"

"They won't insure us."

*Oh now it's "us"?* "Why not?"

"I should be more specific. They won't insure any venture, as they said, that has any connection with you."

"I see."

"Something about respect and the police and, well, the gentleman used much more colorful language."

"I bet he did."

"So here's the thing, Kat. I need you to pay them a visit and smooth things over."

"Why can't we just go with some other firm?"

"Did I mention they're the cheapest?"

"Jordan, there's gotta be—"

"Kat?"

"Yes?"

"Go talk to him."

# THE POSSESSION OF BLACKSTONE MANSION

Now it was her turn to sigh. "All right. I'll go."

"Attagirl."

"I'll text you any updates."

"I'm sure you will."

She hung up. "Great."

In another few minutes, she was standing outside Blackstone Insurance next to her car at an angle where, she hoped, no one could see her from the inside. She, though, could see the inspirational posters decorating the cubicles inside.

> SUCCESS: HARD WORK + PERSISTENCE

...and...

> MANIFEST TODAY'S DREAMS
> INTO TOMORROW'S REALITY

She had no strategy, had no speech prepared. She had no idea how she was going to get Drew to do anything other than tighten the screws so much that she'd have no choice but to go back to Jordan and beg.

She did not want to do that.

Since Jordan's fortune was bankrolling all of this, she had little wiggle room in which to try his patience. While he hadn't been a mean guy, he had been vindictive enough to show her he was not only capable of being so, but often took pleasure from it.

## AUGUSTINE PIERCE

With a quick exhale, she marched up to Blackstone Insurance's front door and opened it wide. She figured as long as she was going to endure this humiliation, she might as well embrace it.

She sat in one of the reception area's faux-leather chairs. She picked up and thumbed through one of the expired fashion magazines. She heard Drew's muffled voice on the phone back in an office she hadn't yet seen. She didn't listen to the words, but could hear what sounded like somewhat feigned delight. She guessed he was speaking to a customer, one he actually liked, or in the least could stand.

A woman in her twenties with long blonde hair pulled back in a ponytail greeted her. "Good afternoon! Did you have an appointment?"

"Not exactly," Katherine said.

"I see. Well, I'll let Mr. Barrister know you're here. What's your name?"

"Katherine Norrington."

The woman's head twitched to the side as if Katherine's name had rung a bell. "Norrington."

"We've had business in the past."

Most likely not wanting to irritate an established customer, the woman perked right up and headed toward her desk. "Wonderful! I'll let him know."

"Thanks." *Well, here goes.*

The woman returned to her cubicle and emerged with a Post-it note. She marched back to Drew's office, knocked, and quietly opened the door. He stopped talking for a single second, likely long enough to glance at the note, then continued. "No, no, I get ya, man." There was no indication that he was making any effort to end his call.

*Great. Guess I'm gonna be here a while. Glad I already saw Kirk.*

The woman closed the office door and paused by Katherine. "Just one minute."

"Thanks."

The woman smiled and went back to her cubicle.

Katherine half listened to Drew's chat as she took out her phone and played some *Fruit Ninja*. She heard the receiver hang up and felt an adrenaline surge, expecting that he was finally going to come get her. But then she heard a moment of silence.

"Hey, buddy..." Drew started a whole new conversation with someone who sounded like an old, close friend.

*Guess I'll see how far I can get in* Fruit Ninja. *If not that, maybe I'll re-download* Tetris.

A half hour passed as Drew made call after call.

At some point, the woman approached Katherine with an apologetic air. She spoke in a cautious tone. "I'm so sorry. I'm sure it'll be just another minute."

"I'm fine," Katherine reassured her. "Thanks."

The woman brought another note to the office. Drew did not react.

## AUGUSTINE PIERCE

At nearly an hour, it tempted Katherine to tell the woman that she'd come back some other time, but then she reminded herself of Jordan. *He'll just demand that you come back.* As she relaunched *Fruit Ninja* for at least the thirtieth time, she heard Drew's voice.

"Katherine J. Norrington," he said.

*What's with the J? Is that supposed to be some kind of dad joke? Like he calls everyone that?* She put her phone in her pocket and stood up. She offered her hand. "Drew."

He did not shake her hand. "Why don't you come on back? Let's have a chat."

His use of "chat" reminded her of her grade school principal, who used it in the same way, as in "I'm going to scold you for twenty minutes and you're going to listen."

She followed him back to his office. On his desk, she noticed two framed pictures. One was of him and a frumpy, middle-aged brunette with fireworks exploding behind them. The other, much older photograph was of a man who strongly resembled Drew and a little boy, both holding up a huge fish they'd caught.

Drew closed the door. "Please, have a seat."

Katherine sat. She wasn't sure if she should begin the barrage of apologies now or wait for a more obvious in.

"So, you're looking to insure a piece of commercial property," he said.

"Well, technically, I'm not the one insuring it."

"Funny. I don't recall asking for technicalities."

*Great, he's nitpicking with this level of nitpicks. This oughta go swimmingly.* "Yes, we would like to insure a piece of commercial property."

"And you're only looking to do so for six months?"

"We're flexible, but yes."

"I'm surprised Cameron and Associates is willing to lease for that brief of a time."

"Like I say, we're flexible."

"Well, I don't know if I can do that, Katherine."

"Why not, Drew?"

"As a former landlord of yours—"

"Residential."

"I beg your pardon?"

"You were my residential landlord, not commercial."

"I'm well aware of that, Katherine."

"Just that there's a difference in law and all that."

"I'm well aware of that too. May I finish or would you prefer to keep interrupting me?"

*Maybe I can find a dentist to extract some teeth later.* "Of course. I apologize."

"What I was going to say, before you interrupted me, was that as a former landlord of yours, I know a little bit about your reliability as a tenant."

She waited for him to continue. She suspected he was hoping she'd interrupt so that he could crab about that some more.

"And I can say"—he finally continued—"is that your reliability makes me hesitant in issuing a policy."

"May I interject?"

"Go right ahead."

"If it's any help, the fact of Cameron and Associates being paid their rent won't have anything to do with me. It'll come from Jordan Blackstone, most likely from his office of attorneys or other serfs he has in his charge."

"Serfs?"

"You won't have to deal with me directly or even indirectly. The check'll go out and that'll be it."

Drew kicked back in his seat. "Hm. Well, that certainly is reassuring, but I don't know. My gut's just not feelin' it."

*If I have to go back to Jordan empty-handed...* "Drew, can we be honest with each other?"

"That's my favorite state of being."

"I know you don't like me."

"I never said I don't like you, Katherine."

"Please, don't interrupt me."

The right corner of his mouth lifted in a little admiring grin.

"You don't like me, and I'm almost completely neutral to you. The only reason Jordan Blackstone wants to go with your firm is that he's a rich prick who's also a cheap prick," she said.

"Is there any other kind?"

She chuckled, and didn't remind him about interrupting. "He can go elsewhere, but probably won't. So you got me. Fine. How can we make this work?"

Drew's eyebrows lifted in an expression of thorough self-satisfaction. "Well, to be perfectly honest with you, Katherine..."

"Yes?"

"I don't know that we can."

She leaned forward, resting her elbows on his desk. "Drew," she repeated, "how can we make this work?"

His expression relaxed, hopefully now taking her seriously. "What do you propose?"

"Your father and you—"

"I dunno that you wanna bring my daddy into this." He indirectly referred to the occasion when, only weeks ago, she'd had Kirk and his crew move a giant pile of furniture and firearms from the mansion into the first floor of Drew's late father's house. Specifically against Drew's wishes. When Drew had discovered the antiques taking up almost the entire floor, things had gotten tense.

"Just hear me out. Please."

He nodded for her to continue.

"Your father and you used to go fishing. If I'm right, some of the happiest memories from your childhood."

Drew offered a simple, much slower nod, most likely intrigued by where she was going with this.

"How would you like it if the Blackstone Family Trust made a sizable donation, in your father's name, to the..." She searched her memory of various nearby areas. "Tualatin Valley..."

"Wildlife Conservation Fund?"

She nodded. "To ensure that future generations can enjoy the rivers, creeks, and other waterways as much as you and your father did?"

Drew leaned forward. "How sizable?"

"More than your father could've done."

Drew nodded slowly, letting the offer really sink in.

"Again, in his name," she confirmed.

"I'd say that'd be a mighty fine gesture on the part of the Blackstone family."

"Fine enough to issue a policy and perhaps accept my sincerest apologies for our previous tensions?"

"You make this happen, Katherine, the only tension I'll feel is what creeps up my lower back every night before bed."

"I bet I could get Jordan to recommend a masseuse. Say, at a sizable discount?"

# 6

"How much?" Jordan sounded like his head was about to explode.

"It's either that or we go somewhere else." Katherine started her car.

"That much, and I might as well start my own insurance company."

"It's not *that* much."

He sighed.

"It's a write-off," she said.

"Yeah."

"It'll help your standing in the community."

"Didn't realize I needed community standing."

"And anywhere else will be much more expensive without the benefit of some greased wheels. Drew is connected to a lot of wheels out here."

"Wheels that can make the rest of this whole process run smoother?"

"I don't doubt it." She wrapped up the conversation and drove home. "You gotta be kidding me!" she exclaimed as she pulled up to her building.

# AUGUSTINE PIERCE

A giant bouquet of a delirious assortment of flowers—red and white roses, sunflowers, and violets among them—sat on the doorstep.

She parked haphazardly, nearly outside the line, jumped out, and ran up to the door. She now saw that the bouquet had a card with her name on it. "Seriously, Luke? Flowers?" She tried to pick up the bouquet. It was very heavy. "Great. So now I gotta lug it in!"

She opened the door and half picked up, half dragged the bouquet inside. "Thank God for elevators!"

Reaching her floor, she dragged the bouquet to her door, opened it, and awkwardly moved the bouquet inside while holding the door open. She carried the bouquet to her kitchen island and dumped it there precariously near the edge. As she stepped away to close the door, she heard paper crinkle and turned around just in time to see the bouquet tip off the island. Her hands shot out, and she caught it. She breathed quickly, grateful not that she'd saved the bouquet, but that she hadn't dumped flowers everywhere, a mess she'd then have to clean up.

Moving the bouquet to the middle of the island, she closed the door, locked it, and returned to the island. She gazed at the bouquet in part amazement and part irritation. The fact was, Luke knew what she liked, and this was easily one of the more beautiful bouquets she'd ever seen. At the same time, she was seriously annoyed that he honestly seemed to think that such a basic gesture would erase everything that had happened between them.

Reluctantly, she opened the card. The paper was lightly fragrant, a very nice touch. A brief message read...

> I'm so sorry, Kat. Please see me.
> —Luke

"Screw you," she told the card. She turned around, intending to toss it, but she hesitated.

She looked down at the text. While she knew that he'd merely ordered the writing and its style, she couldn't help but feel a little softness toward him for the gesture. *What about Kirk?* "Well, of course Kirk!" she declared to herself out loud.

"Sorry, Luke, not good enough," she told the card as she tossed it. She felt a little bad. With zero intention of calling, texting, or e-mailing him, she knew he'd sit around whatever hotel room he'd checked into and wonder. But he'd hurt her so much.

Facing the bouquet, she stared at it long and hard. She shook her head. "It'd be a shame to let it go completely to waste." She picked it up and, with great effort, carried it to her coffee table. "Hopefully, it'll get enough light." As she stood away from it, she had to admit that it looked really nice providing such color in the middle of her living space. "Really is pretty." *Okay, you can enjoy it for a day or two, but then you gotta toss it.* And certainly before she got Kirk to come over. *That'd be so awkward.*

Retiring to her bedroom, she lay down. She wasn't sure what to do to fill the rest of the week. She'd already set up as much as she could, leading up to moving the rest of the mansion's pieces. With those chores out of the way, nothing else was left but peace and quiet. Ironically, that was all she'd sought when she'd chosen to move from New York to the tiniest burg she could find in rural Oregon. But now that she'd been here several weeks, she was wondering if there was such a thing as too much peace and quiet.

Maybe she'd spend the rest of the week very leisurely getting to know Creek. After all, her sort of boyfriend did live there. She hoped she could discover some hidden-gem bookstore or coffee shop.

*That pendant*, she thought, and her eyes drifted to her bedroom door. Getting out of bed, she went to the living room, and stared at her purse as if it contained the greatest treasure in the world, hers for the taking. She sat, eagerly opened it, and hungrily stuffed her hands into the black bag.

She held the piece reverentially in her palms. Somehow, it didn't feel as heavy this time. She lifted it up to the light to better see its details. As with her flashlight in the mansion, the metal didn't reflect her apartment's lights at all. She turned it at various angles to see if she simply wasn't catching it. Nope. No highlights.

She traced her index finger along the platinum vein that ran through the center of each bar. She moved her finger along the edge, all around the triangle, down one side of the V that stabbed through it. When her fingertip reached the circle attached to the V's point, she flicked it off in a flourish as if she had just tested the sharpness of the mightiest sword ever forged right before she was about to ride off into the battle that would decide the fate of the world.

"What *are* you?" she asked the pendant.

It didn't answer.

"Did they find you? Make you?"

The pendant was silent.

She turned it over and over in her hands. "You don't look like anything I've ever seen. And I've seen a lot." She placed it on her coffee table. Its black contrasted strikingly against the table's white.

She leaned over and examined it as if looking at it through a case in a jewelry store. "Someone wore you. At least that was the intent. But not as jewelry. More as status. No, a declaration. You were declaring something to your owner, and, more importantly, to others. But to whom? What? And why?"

It frustrated her that her normally encyclopedic knowledge of almost every kind of antique simply didn't apply here. It was as if she were peering into the deep end of a lake at night. She knew there was a bottom, maybe even knew the depth, but she could not see it.

She sat up. "I should call Miles. He'll either be able to identify it or know someone who can." Miles Holbrook was a London-based friend with whom she'd done a lot of business over the years. She'd most recently had him come out to Blackstone to sell him Vernon's prized firearms collection. While that deal hadn't gone through, she knew Miles could help her out now.

She picked up the pendant, put it back in its bag, and slid it into her purse. She made sure it was snug and took out her phone to call Miles. Seeing it was 2:00 in the afternoon, she paused. "Crap. It's, like, 11:00 over there."

*That metal.* "I wonder." On her phone, she googled metallurgy Portland area. One firm came up in Milwaukie, a nearby suburb of Portland. Nemako Metallurgical Services. She gave their site a quick look over and sent an e-mail.

With the pendant's shape and its metal properties swimming around in her head, she put her phone away, made herself some dinner, watched a documentary on the history of gold in jewelry, and went to bed.

## 7

Katherine was up at 8:00. She chose not to get dressed yet, rather eat breakfast first. She was walking out of the hallway when something caught the bottom of her peripheral vision.

Rot.

She looked down. A small pile of dried, rotted petals and leaves had piled up in the space right next to the bouquet. She scooped up the pile and tossed it in the garbage. She checked the flowers. The very edge of the bouquet had fallen off overnight. It was a small enough portion that it was almost unnoticeable against the rest of the arrangement.

She checked the bouquet's position relative to the living room windows. It seemed to catch enough light. She sniffed, but smelled nothing obvious. No scent of rotting meat or vegetables.

Letting her eyes linger on the bouquet, she went to the kitchen to fix herself some breakfast. Her hunger soon overtook her curiosity, and as she ate, she forgot about the mysterious rotting flowers.

# THE POSSESSION OF BLACKSTONE MANSION

After breakfast, she got dressed. Part way through, her phone *buzzed*. She checked it to see that Nemako Matallurgical had sent an e-mail. Mr. Nemako was welcoming her to bring the pendant in this morning for a look.

---

Katherine was on her way to Nemako a little after 9:00. She dictated to her phone. "Text Kirk..."

> Re Sat, thinking same bat time, same bat place. Can't wait for Fri. :)

She patted her purse, sitting in the passenger's seat. She could feel the pendant's hard edges through the purse's cloth. *Phew!* This was at least the tenth time she'd checked. At least. More likely the thirtieth. She didn't know why, but she felt far more protective of this piece than she had even of Gloria Blackstone's jewelry box she'd found in the mansion's master bedroom. For all Katherine knew, the pendant was worthless, other than its in-laid platinum. She didn't know its history. She didn't even know which family member had owned it, though she suspected, given where she'd found it, it was probably the family's earliest patriarch, Silas. Yet there was something about the object that made her feel protective, even possessive over it.

She soon reached Nemako, a small, boxy industrial building a few blocks off Milwaukie's main drag. She scooped up her purse, exited her car, and headed for the front door. As she was about to reach for the handle, she felt a distinct chill at the back of her neck. It was similar to the ones that had presaged spirits, but... "I'm nowhere near the mansion," she told herself as she rubbed her neck. She turned around.

No one was there. Only the occasional passerby farther up the street. She held out her hand, but no breeze tickled her fingertips. She ignored the sensation, at least for the moment, as she went inside.

She reached the tiny reception area where a middle-aged woman looked up and smiled at her. "Good morning!"

"'Morning. Katherine Norrington to see Mr. Nemako."

"I'll let him know you're here."

"Thanks." Katherine stepped away.

"Ms. Norrington," a booming male voice welcomed.

Katherine turned around to see a tall, barrel-chested man in coveralls. His name badge read Jake. "'Morning, Mr. Nemako."

Jake gave her a dismissive wave. "Mr. Nemako's the old man. Call me Jake." He offered his large, calloused hand.

## THE POSSESSION OF BLACKSTONE MANSION

Katherine shook hands. "No problem. Call me Kat."

"Kat, I understand you have a rather remarkable piece for me."

Katherine opened her purse and carefully took out the pendant's bag. *Why are you being so...? Not like it's gonna break.* She peeled back the black cloth so he could see the pendant, but didn't actually hand it over. *Let him see it!* She ignored her inner voice.

"Would you look at that? Where did you say you found this?"

"I'm curating the Blackstone estate. Found it in the mansion."

"Blackstone estate?"

"Yeah, an old lumber family. Mansion's in Blackstone, near Mt. Hood, but the heir lives in Portland."

"Huh," he said, obviously never having heard of any of this. "Well, why don't you come on back?" He waved for her to join him.

She followed him into a workshop area decked out in all kinds of heavy industrial tools. He led her to a little desk with a computer sitting in a nearby corner. He gestured for her to sit on the microscopic, uncomfortable-looking swivel chair. She sat and gently placed her purse and the pendant on her lap. *You're treating it like it's a newborn baby! Even if it falls on the floor, it won't break!*

He sat across from her in another swivel chair and held out his hands. "May I?"

She regarded him as if he'd just asked her to take her pants off. "Um...."

"Closer look?"

She hesitated in handing over the pendant. *What are you waiting for? This is why you came here!* She set the piece in his outstretched hands.

"Funny symbol."

"Yeah."

"What's it mean?"

Even though she didn't know, and didn't care that he knew she didn't know, she suddenly didn't want to answer him. "I'm not sure."

"Huh, yeah. Appears to be one piece."

"What do you mean?"

"No solder marks. No bending creases."

"What does that...?"

"It's very common, in artistic pieces like this..."

*Artistic. I hadn't thought of it as an objet d'art.*

"Where you have these various components coming together"—he pointed to the triangle's corners—"for each of these sides to actually be a separately fashioned part. Then the craftsman, or woman, he glues 'em together, so to speak."

"What's it mean that someone didn't glue it together?"

"Well, in the least that it was a complex job, required a lot of care, high skill. I mean, even if they poured the metal into a mold, gotta fashion the mold, heat the metal. Oh wait a minute."

"What's that?"

"If they poured it into a mold... There's no sign of it."

"What do you mean?"

"No mold's perfect. You always have some mark or seam, evidence that the craftsman, or woman, had to sorta scrape off any excess. But this piece"—he held it up so she could see what he was talking about—"is uniform all around. No sign of any seams."

"So, how did they make it?"

He turned the pendant over and over in his hands, inspecting every square centimeter. "I am not sure."

"You know what kind of metal it is?"

"Off the top of my head? Could be zirconium. That's the only naturally black metal there is. No idea why anyone would wanna make a necklace outta that."

"It's not a necklace." Her tone was far harsher than she intended. *Who cares what he calls it?*

He stared at her. "Oh, uh, 'course not." He grinned sheepishly.

"I just mean it's not a traditional necklace. More of a pendant."

"Gotcha. Well, like I say, could be zirconium, but we'd have to do some tests to zir-o in." He grinned.

"What kind of tests?"

"Magnetism test, spark test, Mohs hardness."

She was feeling increasingly protective of the pendant. "Will any of those injure the piece?"

"Injure? No. Maybe embarrass it a little." He smiled. She did not, so his smile faded. "Uh, no, with magnetism, we just run a magnet by it. Spark, we whack it with a rock to see if it reacts. Mohs, we test how hard it is by pressing—"

She stood and relieved the pendant from his hands. "Thank you, Mr. Nemako." She quickly wrapped the pendant in its bag and placed it back in her purse. "None of that will be necessary."

He stood. "No problem, Ms. Norrington. Uh..." He looked like he didn't quite know what was happening now.

She helped him out by starting for the door.

"Well, you need anything else, you give us a ring," he said.

She didn't answer at first. *Won't know what kind of metal it is without letting him test it. Shut up.* "Uh, yeah, thanks." She walked straight out of the building before they could exchange any more pleasantries.

As she reached her car, her phone *buzzed*. It was a text from Kirk.

> All good. Looking forward to Fri too.

# THE POSSESSION OF BLACKSTONE MANSION

The second she got home, she placed her purse on the sofa, tore off her jacket, and grabbed a beer out of the refrigerator. She popped it open and downed a good few gulps. She plopped onto the sofa and set the bottle on the coffee table.

She picked up her purse, took out the pendant, and turned it over and over in her hands. Where before she'd felt a strong curiosity toward it, now she was feeling... need. The compulsion rose within her to throw that silver chain over her neck and never take it off. *Huh. Weird. I've worn expensive jewelry before, but never felt like this.*

She set the pendant on the coffee table next to her beer. She took out her phone and dialed Miles. She was a little nervous as it was already evening in London, and she didn't want to interrupt his dinner. But she had to learn more.

He picked up quickly. "Katherine! How are you? Ready to sell me more antique guns?"

She smiled. "Not today, Miles. Though more pieces will be available soon enough. Already took a good look at Mr. Blackstone's music room."

"Rock on! Can't wait!"

"I'm actually calling to ask a small favor."

"Ooh," he feigned concern, "not so sure about that."

"Yeah, yeah. It's tiny. I just need some info."

## AUGUSTINE PIERCE

"Sorry I can't help, love. I may be British, but I've no idea where you can find the best fish and chips in London."

"Ha ha. No, I found a"—she suddenly realized she didn't know how to describe the pendant, so went with the most basic—"piece. It's a little out of my purview."

"Out of *your* purview? How is that even possible?"

"Well, this one is. I'm gonna text you a pic. Lemme know what you think?"

"Certainly happy to help."

She positioned the pendant on the coffee table, with plenty of white space around it for the clearest image. She took a quick picture and texted it. "You get it?"

"Just now. Huh. Where'd you find this? The basement of some long-dead D&D cosplayer?"

"Right? No, I found it in Blackstone mansion, where I've been working."

"Wait. The place where you found the guns?"

"The same."

"Yeah, I dunno that I can make head or tails of it, but I might know someone who can. Mate who works in antiquities. Name's Nigel. Anybody knows old, odd crap, it's him."

*Don't call it crap, Miles! Whoa, Kat, chill!*

"Mind if I give him your number?"

"Not at all. Number, e-mail."

"All right. Yeah, I'll give him a ring, send him the pic, and tell him to reach out to you."

"Thanks, Miles. Really appreciate it."

"No problem. Just don't forget me when you're ready with more of that mansion's goodies."

"I will. I will. Or rather, I won't. Forget you." She grinned.

"Oh, and Kat?"

"Yeah?"

"About Nigel. He's a little... eccentric."

"All right."

"Just, you know, keep that in mind."

"Gotcha. Thanks. Cheers."

"Cheers, love."

They hung up. She set her phone on the coffee table, picked up her beer, and downed another few healthy gulps. She set down the bottle, picked up the pendant, and held it close. She spoke to it as she turned it over and over in her hands. "What are you? Where did you come from?"

## 8

Katherine came to around 9:30 Wednesday morning. She got up, showered, dressed, and was headed out when she saw an even bigger pile of rotten petals and leaves on her coffee table and surrounding floor. She stopped and gazed at it. The entire bouquet had rotted away. *What happened here?* She anxiously dusted the floral remains off the pendant and was relieved to see that they hadn't tarnished it.

She picked up the pendant and put it safely away in her purse. She dumped the petal pile in the garbage. She eyed the rest spread out on the floor around the table. She sighed as she went to the hallway closet and took out a broom and dustpan. She made quick, if not at all thorough, work of the mess.

She finally headed out to Creek's downtown area. It was much bigger than Blackstone's and, frankly, much more interesting. There were lots of cute little shops, cafés, and galleries that surrounded several blocks of park area. As she drove around taking in

## THE POSSESSION OF BLACKSTONE MANSION

all the local color, she spotted an establishment that made her hit the brakes.

A jewelry store.

Without another second of consideration, she parked in a nearby spot, snatched her purse, got out, and ran inside.

The store had a handful of display cases with handsome, if not fashionable, jewelry. There were even a few chunky diamond rings. Nothing as impressive as the emerald-and-diamond set once owned by Gloria Blackstone, which Katherine had discovered in the mansion weeks ago, but then again, she'd never seen anything quite like Gloria's set.

Katherine approached the main counter. A short man with wispy white hair emerged from a back room.

"Good morning, young lady," he said. "Looking for anything in particular? Engagement ring, perhaps?"

"Actually, I was hoping to get a professional opinion."

"Oh?"

She placed her purse on the counter and took out the pendant's bag. She carefully slid the pendant onto the countertop.

"My my," the man said, then looked up at her. "Do you mind?"

*Yes, of course I mind!* "Not at all."

The man picked up the piece and looked it over. "That's some exquisite platinum work. At first glance, I'm guessing... My my, is that ninety-five?"

"I don't know." She intended to sound matter-of-fact, but her tone came out much harsher. She politely lifted the pendant from his fingers.

"Where did you find it?"

"Recovered it from Blackstone mansion, about half hour from here."

"I see. I'm sorry. Please pardon my manners. I'm Gerald. Gerald Brown. This is my humble little shop."

"Hi, Gerald. I'm Katherine Norrington. Please call me Kat."

"If you like, Kat, we can take the piece in back, have a closer look." He pointed to the room behind him.

"Yeah." She nodded and followed him back.

There she found a modest workshop with all kinds of tools for cutting gems, working metal, and a huge magnifying loupe on a mechanical arm.

He gestured for her to sit next to him. "If you could..." He pointed to the pendant.

She held it awkwardly under the loupe.

He offered his hand. "If I might..."

She set it in his hand.

# THE POSSESSION OF BLACKSTONE MANSION

*Thunk!* The pendant dropped straight out of his fingers and hit the table.

*Watch it, dude!*

He chuckled with a twinge of embarrassment. "Hefty little piece, isn't she?"

Katherine didn't answer him. She kept her eyes trained on him as he examined the pendant under the lens.

"Oh yes. Oh yes indeed. My my." He sat back, but continued to stare at the pendant. "Ms. Norrington. Kat." He turned his head to face her, but kept the pendant held under the loupe. "This is easily the finest platinum work I've ever seen."

"Wow."

"Yes. You say you found it at Blackstone mansion?"

"That's right."

"Well, I knew the Blackstone clan was wealthy, but this piece? I mean, the materials, this odd black metal and the platinum, the latter is alone worth many thousands. But the craftsmanship." He looked her in the eyes. "I've never seen anything like it."

"What can you tell me about it? The history?"

"Unfortunately, I don't know that I can. It's not just the quality of the work. I've never seen a piece like this of any kind anywhere. I'm guessing the Blackstones had it custom made. To what end, I couldn't tell you."

"The shape? The symbol?"

"I'm very sorry. I'm not a semiotician."

"Of course." She took back the pendant and stood. "Thank you for your time."

"If you were interested in parting with it, I'm positive I could fetch you a very handsome price."

*No way, dude!* "Uh, thanks, but I'm afraid it's not mine to part with."

"Of course. I understand. Well, thank you for dropping by, allowing me to take a look."

She said goodbye and left. Back in her car, she stared at the pendant under the late-morning light. She couldn't get used to the fact that the black metal reflected nothing, but the platinum's sheen, it was a sight to behold.

Fighting the instinct to gaze at the object all day in her car, she put it back in its bag and slid it into her purse. She then drove home, placed her purse on the end of the sofa, and made some lunch.

During lunch, she kept staring at that bouquet devoid of flowers. She finally got up, mid-chew, and marched over to it. She picked up the remainder of the arrangement and carried it out to the garbage chute next to the elevator. She dumped it down with intense satisfaction and dusted her hands.

# THE POSSESSION OF BLACKSTONE MANSION

The rest of Wednesday had flown right by, and now, Thursday morning, Katherine was in the middle of breakfast when her phone *buzzed*. It was a number she recognized, but couldn't remember. "Hello?"

"Ms. Norrington?" a male voice asked.

"Yes?"

"Hi, this is Dan Cameron."

"Oh yes, of course. Hey, Dan."

"Hey, so we're all good on this end to rent you and Mr. Blackstone that property for Norrington Antiques."

"Great! Uh, so what do you guys need?"

"Only to hand you the keys."

"Wonderful. I can be there in twenty-five to thirty."

He chuckled. "I'm afraid I'm a little farther out. Is thirty-five to forty okay?"

She grinned. "That's no problem. See you soon, Dan."

She drove out to the cream-and-red storefront. It turned out she was a few minutes early. She was waiting by the front door when a giant SUV pulled up and a short man with a brown crew cut got out.

"'Morning!" Dan said.

"'Morning, Mr. Cameron."

"No, no. Please. Dan's fine." He held out his hand. She shook hands. "Then Kat's fine too."

He reached into his coat pocket and took out a set of keys. He didn't hand them to her yet. Instead, he unlocked the store's front door. "Shall we?"

*Is it gonna be that much different inside?* "Yeah, let's."

He held the door open for her. She walked in. To her amazement, the space looked much bigger on the inside than it had on the street. As far as she could tell, it was big enough not only for about two full rooms of the mansion's antiques, but also a little office for her and even an assistant in back. "Excellent."

"Yeah? It'll do?"

She faced him. "I think so."

He held out the keys. She accepted them.

"Well, electricity and heat are on." He walked over to a light switch by the front door. He flipped it. The room's lights flicked on. "You can install your sign whenever you want." He pointed to the window where her hypothetical sign would be painted.

"This is great, Dan. Thanks so much."

"Yeah. If you need anything, anything at all, just call my cell." He handed her a card, then offered his hand again.

She accepted the card and shook his hand. "Perfect."

"Well, I hate to cut this short, but I'm afraid I gotta run."

## THE POSSESSION OF BLACKSTONE MANSION

"No problem. You go. I'll get the lay of the land here."

"Take care, Kat."

"You too, Dan."

He left.

She gave the space a 360, imagining how and where she might display certain pieces. A table here, the picture of Mt. Hood from the Blackstones' gallery there. *Yeah, this'll work.*

She took out her phone and texted not only Miles, but Aleeyah, her New York-based friend with whom she'd done plenty of business, Chase, her LA-based friend, who'd done her last deal, that of Vernon Blackstone's firearms collection, and four more names. She sent them all the same message.

> Almost set up for you to see Blackstone music room pieces. Alert your melodically inclined contacts.

---

Katherine spent the rest of Thursday, and most of Friday, taking care of basics, like grocery shopping, and watching documentaries on the Silk Road. She'd already gotten responses from Aleeyah, Chase, and two others. They were all eager to learn more, and had requested that she keep them up to date. Before she knew it, it was late Friday evening.

## AUGUSTINE PIERCE

She was sitting on her sofa, holding the pendant. She ran her finger along its platinum vein, trying to extract any more sense out of it. Something nagged at the back of her mind. She checked her phone. It was already 6:00. "Oh no! Kirk! I gotta go!"

She dropped the pendant on the coffee table, ran to her bathroom, and checked herself out in the mirror. She groaned in disappointment. "I can't go out like this." She went to her bedroom and started tearing outfits out of her closet. "It's not the opera, Kat. It's bowling. Just pick something." She took off her jeans and shirt, and put on a nicer pair of jeans and a black sweater. She ran back into the living room, put on her coat, grabbed her purse, and opened the door.

Her eyes darted to the pendant. She swiped it, shoved it in her purse, and left.

It was a good twenty minutes to Creek. She may not have been late, but she was pushing it. At minute eighteen, she was in Creek's downtown area. In another minute, she was cruising down the main street nearest to Kirk's place, and in one more minute, she had pulled up to a modest apartment complex with tasteful wrought-iron gates.

She tapped Kirk's number on her phone.

"Hello?" Kirk answered in a feigned surprised tone.

"Hey, sorry I'm late. Lost track of the time."

# THE POSSESSION OF BLACKSTONE MANSION

"Looks to me like you're right on time."

"Still."

"Be down in a sec."

"Great." She hung up and twiddled her thumbs. She was excited. Their second proper date. She felt like she was thirteen all over again and the cutest guy in school was picking her up to go to the dance, except she was the one doing the picking up.

Kirk strode out of his building. He wore a navy blue sweater, dark jeans, and had clearly shaved and done his hair a little.

*He is so hot*. She got out of the car and opened her arms for a hug.

He wrapped his arms around her and held tight for a long second. "You look great!"

"You look even better."

"Ah, this old thing?" He ran his right hand up and down his left sleeve. He started for the passenger side.

"Uh-uh," she faux scolded him as she slipped ahead. She stood by his door like a chauffeur and opened it slowly with her other arm outstretched. "Sir?"

"Wow, such service!" He smiled.

"I asked you."

He got in and she closed his door. She went back to her side, got in, tapped the address into her phone, and started on their way.

"How's it been going? At the mansion?" he asked.

*Right! I never told him about Jordan's little scheduling snafu!* "Going."

"That bad, huh?"

"No, it just... Jordan ordered me out there Monday at the ass-crack of dawn to meet an electrician to assess the, uh, wiring. So you guys don't have to fumble around in the dark."

"I don't mind fumbling."

She grinned. "Well, dude didn't show and—" *I found this weird-ass pendant that neither a metallurgist nor a jeweler can identify. A pendant which I feel oddly protective over. Oddly drawn to.* "And, uh, yeah, didn't show." She didn't want to go into the pendant with him, because she knew she didn't have enough information. Plus, she didn't want to damper their date. "This'll sound strange, but do you mind if we talk about it later?"

"Not strange at all. I don't wanna talk about work either."

She smiled at him. "Why not? What happened?"

He shrugged. "Work stuff."

"Annie?"

"Nah, she's fine. A little distant lately."

*Because I scared her off.* "Really?"

"Yeah, it's weird. We used to be so buddy-buddy, but the last few days, definitely been feelin' a chill."

"Sorry to hear that." *Sorry, not sorry.*

"It's fine. Like I say, work stuff. But that's over. We're gonna have a wonderful night."

"That's right."

"Of me cleaning your clock."

"Oh, in your dreams, son!"

They chit-chatted about little things like the weather, the cold, the rest of the way there. Despite her having asked him that they set her day aside, she couldn't stop thinking about the pendant. That non-reflective black. That bright platinum. That triangle and V.

She was still thinking of that when they pulled into the parking lot of King's Lanes. The establishment was a bit on the grubby side, with dirty off-white walls and a giant orange sign with neon yellow lighting outlining both the K and the L. Having parked, she moved to get out before him and finish her gesture of opening his door, but he beat her to it.

They met in front of the car. He took her hand and squeezed it.

*Oh, God, I'm gonna ride you so hard!* Despite her thoughts, she did her best not to look or sound too eager. "So, this is the place?"

"Indeed it is. They've got a decent deal on hot dogs, fries, beer, and bottomless fountain drinks."

"Can't wait."

They went in and surveyed the scene. There were families, teenagers on dates and in groups, and adults who looked like they were professional bowlers, striking one after the other.

She nodded at a man looking to be in his thirties who struck all ten pins. "Nice."

"Eh, different league." Kirk paused and gave her a goofy grin. "Get it? Different league? Bowling league?"

"Oh my God. Terrible." She laughed so hard she snorted.

"Right?"

"You'd best get me my shoes and feed me."

"Yes, ma'am."

They walked to the shoes area. They each ordered. He took out his card.

"No, no," she said. "Second date. My treat."

"I don't think so."

She put her hand over his, holding his card, and took out her wallet. "Kirk, come on."

"Kat."

"Kirk?"

"How about Dutch?"

"Okay. Get each other's shoes."

"And buy each other's food."

She nodded.

They got their shoes and balls and found an open lane. They set down their bowling gear.

She took her jacket off and hung it over the back of a chair. She set her purse in the middle of the seat so it was in no danger of falling on the ground. She then changed her shoes.

He'd already changed his and was now standing with his hand outstretched. She smiled, took his hand, and they walked to the food area.

They ordered double dogs and fries each, but then he held her hand back when it was time to pay.

"Kirk!" she said.

"You snooze, you don't pay."

"Not how it goes."

He paid. The woman behind the counter got their food. He carried their tray back to their lane.

Katherine dug in to her dogs. "Oh my God! I didn't realize I was so hungry."

"We can always get more."

"If we do, *I'm* buying."

"Sure you are."

They both wolfed down most of their food.

He set up their game, then turned to her. "Ladies first?"

"Man, it's been so long."

"Nothing to worry about. Worst possible thing you can do is fail."

"Wow, you really know how to charm a girl."

"Don't I, though?"

"All right. Here goes." She picked up her ball and jammed her fingers in the order and position where she thought she was supposed to. She waltzed up to the end of their lane and stepped back. Eyeing those pins, she stepped forward and tossed.

The ball bounced twice and rolled into the side.

"Oh my God! You gotta be..." She heard him slow clap behind her.

"That was beautiful."

She faced him. "Oh shut up."

"Seriously, Kat. I mean, I'm gonna have to *try* to do worse."

"Mighty big words, jerk." She grinned and collected her ball.

He picked up his ball. As he passed her, she deftly reached down and gave his butt a gentle pinch.

"Um, excuse me." He turned around and threw her a faux glare. "I'm trying to concentrate."

"Oh I'm sorry!" She smiled.

He smiled back. His eyes hung on her face, lowered, then he faced forward.

*Did he just check out my tits? Kirk, you are not gonna get a wink tonight!*

He rolled. His handling of the ball was far superior to hers, and yet he only knocked down a single pin. He thrust his fists in the air and spun around. "Boo-ya!"

"One lousy pin!"

"I'm sorry. I already forgot. How many did you knock down?"

She stuck out her tongue. "My turn."

"I cannot wait to see this."

"All right, all right."

She felt a chill at the back of her neck.

*What is that?* It was the sensation she'd felt at the mansion more than once, and most recently outside of Nemako Metallurgical. It usually meant the presence of the dead. *But I'm not at the mansion!* She decided it must have been the breeze from someone nearby walking past them. She looked. She saw no one having just walked by. *Must be the air conditioning.* "Hey, you feel that?"

He retrieved his ball. "Only your impending defeat."

"No, I..." She ignored it. For now. She faced the lane, lined up her shot, and rolled the ball. Thankfully, this time it didn't bounce, but it still rolled straight to the side.

"Oh!" He chuckled.

That chill still lingered in her thoughts, but she responded in kind. "It's only defeat when I give up."

"Hey, whatever you need to tell yourself."

She faced him. "You'd better watch it."

He leaned forward. "Or?"

"Or somebody might not get dessert tonight?"

He sounded way too eager. "I didn't know that was on the menu!"

She giggled. He laughed. She picked up her ball.

He rolled. He knocked down another pin. "Man, I am on a *streak!*"

She rolled her eyes. "Yeah, yeah."

"Oh no, please, just try and defeat me now." He strutted back to collect his ball.

She walked up to the lane. "Okay, lane, I don't like you, and you don't like me. But if you let me have this one, I'll..."

"Maybe you should offer the lane a bribe."

"Quiet, you." She turned to face him and wag her finger.

Dark gray. Solid. Directly in front of her. In her personal space. Curves and wrinkles. Flesh. Bone. She was staring at a wall of desiccated flesh stretched over a rib cage. The flesh was long dead and leathery, as if it had been mummified for decades.

Her eyes lifted, an unconscious desire to see who, or what, this was towering over her.

Two black holes. Empty sockets. A sharply triangular nasal hole jutted out right below. Patches of more dark leathery flesh stretched tightly over the hole's edges, over knobby cheek bones, all across the rest of the skull. A jawbone full of black teeth grinned viciously.

Katherine could feel her fingers release her ball. Off in the distance, she heard it *smack* the floor.

The sockets suddenly inflamed with ember red. The jawbone creaked open. Its jerking movements accompanied a deep, gravelly, raspy groan that stabbed into her ears.

And that stench. The worst, most pungent odor. She hadn't smelled anything that awful since her first encounter with Eileen's ghost. The stink scraped at Katherine's sinuses and churned her stomach.

She shrieked so loud it rang in her ears.

9

A hand clasped Katherine's right shoulder. "Katherine! Hey!" Kirk said.

Her eyes snapped to the right. His deeply concerned face stared down at her.

"I... I..." She couldn't think of what to say. She instinctively looked back to her left, where the mummified corpse had stood. Had growled.

The space was empty. There was no sign of it. There was, however, a crowd of very concerned-looking patrons. Wide eyes. Slack jaws. All staring at Katherine.

"I..." she said.

"Ma'am?" a male voice asked.

Her eyes found the kind face of a man in his fifties. He wore a King's Lanes jersey. He was probably the manager.

"Ma'am, you okay?" he asked.

"I..." She reached to her right. She felt Kirk take her hand. She touched his face. "I need to go. I'm sorry."

"Yeah. Of course." Kirk spoke to the manager. "Can you guys, uh...?" He pointed to both their bowling balls and their mid-game score sheet.

"Not a problem, sir. You take care of her."

"Come here, Katherine." Kirk sat her down.

"I need to go." She could feel the tears dripping down her cheeks. *No! So embarrassing!*

"I know. I know. Just gotta get your shoes off."

She felt pressure on her feet as his fingers raced to remove her bowling shoes as quickly as possible. She then felt the slight cool of her shoeless feet. Finally, she felt his hands awkwardly put her shoes on and tie them.

"Here we go." He helped her to her feet.

The next several minutes were a blur. She was aware of being walked out to the parking lot. She was aware of being sat in her car's passenger side. "My purse."

"It's at your feet with your coat."

"Where are we going?"

"Taking you back to your place."

"Will you stay with me?"

"Absolutely, Kat. Of course."

"Please stay with me."

"I'm not goin' anywhere."

She felt his hand squeeze hers. They were silent the rest of the way.

# AUGUSTINE PIERCE

"He... It..." Katherine didn't know how to describe the horrifying creature she'd seen before her. Or rather, she didn't want to. It had taken so much for Kirk to take her seriously with her contact with Eileen Byrne's ghost that to have to mention this new one seemed an impossible task.

"Shh, you don't have to talk." Kirk placed a mug of chamomile tea in front of her.

She didn't quite remember how they'd gotten to her apartment, let alone her sofa, though she had a vague memory of being in her car.

He kept a polite distance. She didn't know whether he was doing so because she'd freaked him out or because he thought she needed the space. She chose to believe the latter.

She couldn't blame him, though. For being freaked out. From his point of view, they'd been right in the middle of flirtatious banter when she'd had a full-on mental breakdown. She guessed that having seen that was nearly as shocking as what she'd seen.

What had she seen? A skeletal specter. Who was he? Why had she seen him?

"Kat," Kirk began, "just to let you know, you don't have to talk if you don't want. We can just sit here. If you can do one thing for me, though?"

She turned her head to him, but said nothing.

"Drink your tea?" he asked.

She nodded, faced forward, and lifted the mug to her lips. The warmth was a wonderful sensation compared to the chill she'd felt right before the ghost had appeared. She swallowed a gulp. Too much. She coughed a little at the gag reflex.

"You okay?" he asked.

She nodded. *The ghost. Okay, let's walk through this.* "He could've been Vernon, Reginald, or Marcus. At least I think. Those are the last family members I know of who lived at the mansion before it was abandoned."

Kirk's tone was deliberate and cautious. "You're saying you saw one again? A ghost?"

"One of the Blackstones. Most likely. Probably. I dunno. Can't be sure."

"Gotcha."

"I don't... I don't understand how he could contact me outside the mansion. Eileen only contacted me inside."

"And no one else saw him."

She turned to Kirk. "You're right. Only I saw him and *outside* the mansion." *The pendant.* "Hand me my purse?"

"Sure." Kirk sounded very confused as he passed her purse to her.

She set down her tea, opened her purse, and took out the pendant.

He dropped his quiet tone. "Oh my God! What the hell is that?"

"I have no idea. I found it in the mansion shortly after Jordan told me the electrician wasn't showing."

"With you so far."

"After I got off the phone, I figured I'd look around, find some potential rooms for us. To move."

"Right. Very considerate."

"I wandered into a tucked-away study, private library, whatever. That's where I found this." She held up the pendant.

"You think there's some connection."

She shook her head. "Maybe?"

"Wow." His tone told her that this was a lot to take in.

"I'm sorry. We don't need to keep talking about this. In fact, I'd prefer not to."

"I don't mind."

"No, I just wanna... Will you go to bed with me?" She winced. "I'm sorry. I did not mean it to sound like that."

He laughed. "It's fine, Kat. I'm happy to sleep next to you."

"Thanks."

He stood and reached out for her hands. She set the pendant on the coffee table. Her gaze lingered.

# THE POSSESSION OF BLACKSTONE MANSION

*Deal with it tomorrow.* She accepted his hands. He lifted her to her feet. They walked arm-in-arm to her bedroom.

There, she started to take off her sweater and jeans. He turned away.

"No, look, please," she said. "Helps me feel safe."

He nodded and faced her.

She stripped down to her bra and underwear. She felt warm and comfortable under his gaze. "Now you."

He grinned bashfully. "Yes, ma'am." He took off his clothes down to his underwear.

She picked up her pants and took out her phone. She set the alarm for early enough that they'd have plenty of time to get ready and meet his guys the next morning. She set the phone on her nightstand.

She held out her hand. He accepted it. She led him to her bed, where she peeled back the comforter and slid inside. She kept his hand in hers as she did so. He pulled the comforter up over them and kissed her hand.

"'Night, Kirk."

"'Night, Kat."

But Katherine's night wasn't over. Not by a long shot. Every time she closed her eyes, she saw that specter's skull. Its red eyes. That horrible stench lingered at the back of her throat, at the base of her sinuses. She eventually passed out, but she came to what seemed like every handful of seconds. It was like enduring a fever dream. The only genuine relief she got was when she saw the sun was rising.

## 10

The alarm blasted Katherine awake what felt like only two minutes later. "Kirk?"

"Mm?" he asked groggily.

"Just wanted to make sure."

He squeezed her. "Still here."

"We should probably get up, shouldn't we?"

"Probably."

"Want breakfast?"

"Absolutely."

They got up. He threw on yesterday's clothes. She put on a fresh sweater and pair of jeans. They went out to the kitchen for a simple breakfast. She kept staring at the pendant on the coffee table.

"What are you thinking?" he asked between bites.

"Wondering if I should keep it with me. If it did… connect me to the ghost, I dunno that I wanna keep it around everywhere. But at the same time"—she eyed him for reassurance—"I don't think I wanna just leave it sitting there."

"You asking me?"

"Yeah."

"If that thing is what you think, you'd probably rather keep an eye on it than not."

She nodded and stood from the dining room table. She picked up the pendant, placed it inside her purse, zipped it up, and slung it over her shoulder. "Keep an eye."

They soon finished breakfast and went out to her car.

On strapping in, she exhaled sharply. "They're probably gonna tease us for arriving together."

"Probably."

"You don't mind?"

"Let 'em tease."

She agreed with a nod and started the car. It was a good twenty minutes before they reached Blackstone mansion's gate.

Three trucks had already arrived. Shane and Dennis were among them. They'd been half of the group who'd helped recover Eileen's remains. True to Katherine's prediction, the instant she and Kirk got out of her car, the guys started up.

"Look who decided to show!" Shane said.

"We're right on time, jerk," Kirk said.

"Shocking, considering what you probably got up to last night," Dennis said.

"All right, guys. Ha ha. Time to reel it in. That's our boss we're talking about," Kirk said with a smile, though his tone was serious.

"Oh, let 'em have one more," Katherine said, trying to keep the mood light.

"When's the wedding?" Shane blurted.

"She gave you one more, and that's what you go with?" Dennis sounded genuinely annoyed.

Two more trucks pulled up.

"That'll be Ross and Mac," Shane said.

The trucks parked and two guys, both in goatees and flannels, got out.

Katherine was already concerned that it was going to be tough to tell all these guys apart.

"My mans!" Dennis cheered as he walked over to greet the new arrivals.

Ross, Mac, and Dennis joined the others and Kirk made introductions.

"I'm so sorry. I will definitely not remember all you guys," Katherine said.

"That's okay, Ms. Norrington. I can't even tell us apart," Mac said.

Everyone laughed.

"Kat, please," Katherine said.

"That I can remember," Ross joked.

They all chatted for a few more minutes as the remaining five arrived. Kirk passed out walkie-talkies while making the last introductions.

Katherine welcomed them all. "Thank you guys for coming out here. I don't know how much Kirk's told you. It's a big job, but a simple one. Likely all weekend, and maybe a few more. We're just surveying, which will pretty much be only me. Then preparing, which will involve protecting the pieces, moving 'em out, loading 'em up. And finally transporting 'em back to my place in town."

She pointed to the mansion. "As you can kinda see from here, it's an enormous place. That means a lot of pieces to move. Care of those pieces is of the utmost importance, so if we only move a couple rooms a day, even if only one, that's fine. Mr. Blackstone, the property's owner, understands that and has granted me permission to handle it. Uh, I'll take lunch orders about 11:00, then drive in to town to pick 'em up." She paused, trying to think of anything else. "I think that's it. Any questions?" She glanced around the group.

Everyone shook their heads.

"All right, great. Uh, remember, cell coverage is crap all over the hill, so if you wanna make a call, you'll have to head farther down the road." She pointed.

"Well, let's get to it. If you'll follow me up the hill..." She pointed to the cobblestone road past the gate.

The group got moving. It was a leisurely hike up the hill, during which Katherine heard curious banter among some of the men about everything from the creepy gate to the cobblestones on which they currently strode, to the huge haunted mansion that loomed before them.

She grinned as they commented on the mansion being haunted. *If you only knew.*

"What's so funny?" Kirk asked with his own little grin.

"Oh nothing. Just heard one of them observe something about all this that I'd thought myself."

Kirk nodded, but didn't pursue the matter.

The group soon arrived at the front doors. Katherine stopped there and faced them. She took out her flashlight and clicked it on. "Here we are, guys. First door to the right of the stairs, then the second door after that. The music room. Some furniture, a harpsichord, lots to be careful of. After me." She walked in.

The guys who hadn't seen the place yet all let out a collective, impressed "whoa."

"Looks even bigger on the inside," Ross observed.

"Probably has to do with how the staircase cuts through the space," Katherine suggested.

The guys grunted their agreement as they continued to take in the area.

Katherine opened the music room's door and shone her flashlight inside.

"Wow," Mac said, on laying his eyes on the jaw-dropping luxury.

"Right?" Kirk asked.

"Who *were* these people?" Ross asked.

"Very wealthy," Katherine said.

"No kidding."

"Guess we should go ahead and set up the lights?" Katherine asked Kirk.

"Yeah. Sam?" Kirk asked a so far mostly silent man in the back who wore a beard and flannel.

As Katherine watched Kirk's and Sam's exchange over the lights, she realized that it really was going to be a challenge to keep these guys straight throughout the day.

"So Kirk says you're an antiques dealer?" Mac asked Katherine while they all waited for the lights to be set up.

"That's right."

"Like *Antiques Roadshow?*"

"Basically. I tend to deal with more obscure, upmarket pieces than them, but yeah, same principle."

"'Cause I got this watch from my granddaddy. Probably not worth much, but if you had a minute..." Mac stopped when he noticed something past her shoulder.

Katherine turned to see Kirk beckoning Mac over.

"'Scuse me," Mac told Katherine. He walked to Kirk, who spoke to him in a hushed tone. Mac nod-

## THE POSSESSION OF BLACKSTONE MANSION

ded. "Sorry, man." He crossed back to Katherine with a shamefully dipped head. "Sorry, ma'am—Uh, Ms. Norrington. Kat."

"Not a problem." But Mac had already walked away before she'd finished her sentence.

Kirk joined her.

"What was that?" she asked.

"I told him your assessing his watch was a few steps below your pay grade and inappropriate given your professional relationship to him."

She shrugged. "Eh, would've taken two seconds."

"Yeah, but then they all would've lined up."

She nodded. "Good point. Good looking out, Mr. Whitehead." *That was awfully protective of him.*

He smiled and rejoined Sam and the others, setting up the lights. After another few minutes, Sam switched them on. They blasted their rays all over the entryway and music room. Under such intense illumination, the contents of both spaces looked even more luxurious. The reds and yellows popped off the walls. The sofas and chairs looked like supermodels might lounge on them at any moment, ready for high-fashion photographers to snap their shutters. The entryway's twin archer statues, Artemis and Apollo, looked like they might leap from their pedestals and battle to the death.

Katherine shuddered a little at seeing the harpsichord. *Hope they're careful in here.* She waved the guys over. "Gather 'round, boys! So as you can see, very fragile stuff. I know you will be, but please be very careful. As I told some of you already, even one nick on a corner can cost Mr. Blackstone ten thousand, so it's imperative we take great care of these pieces."

The guys nodded and agreed.

"All right. I'll get outta your way," Katherine said.

The guys acknowledged and got to work. They started packing the room's items in Bubble Wrap and blankets, and moving them out. Kirk had recruited well, as they were all careful and efficient. Katherine roughly calculated that at the rate they were going, this room might not even take a full day.

She hovered for about two minutes, watching them pack one side table and one sofa. She also looked on as they carried those items out of the room, through the entryway, and down the hill. Satisfied that they'd be able to handle themselves, she left them to it.

She entered the door to the left of the entryway staircase. As she walked down the dark, echoing hallway, she felt just as creeped out as she had the very first time she'd set foot in the house.

She opened the first door, the gallery. There hung the various family portraits that she'd first seen only weeks ago. There were individual portraits of Reginald, Marcus, and Vernon, and then one group picture of the whole family, including the matriarch, Gloria.

Katherine studied the boys' portraits with her flashlight. "Which one of you was it?" She turned to Vernon's picture, in which he leaned on a cane with his left hand while the right rested on a rifle. The moment her flashlight grazed the lower half of his face, she felt a jolt of adrenaline. *Those cheekbones.* Her light drifted up the rest of his face. She nodded at the eyes. Even though the ones she'd seen had only been sockets, those shapes... The resemblance was unmistakable. She was certain of it. *What were you doing outside the mansion, Vernon?* And why wasn't he here now? She looked around just to be sure, but saw no movement, no shadow in a shadow, as she'd discovered during one of her first visits to the mansion.

She exited the gallery and headed to the west tower. She paused where the corridor in which she stood met the west-east hallway. She shone her light to the left and right as if about to cross a very busy street.

The beam fell upon the sculpted black marble face of the bust she'd seen the first time she'd visited. That of Silas Blackstone. He was Vernon's grandfather, if she remembered correctly. The sculpture barely poked out of its niche in the wall. Such a position made it look like it was sneaking around in the dark.

She walked up to it and examined the face, with its brushed-back hair, deep eye sockets, and long, pointy nose.

Finally stepping away from Silas's bust, she wondered again why it had been so prominently featured here. It was such a point of focus with respect to the rest of the mansion she'd seen.

When she reached the end of the hall, the west tower, she paused on entering. She hadn't been here since she and Kirk's team had dug into the masonry below the floor boards to discover Eileen Byrne's body.

And what a discovery that had been. Not only had her corpse laid under several feet of masonry, but someone had placed it in an elaborate, lidless, concrete coffin with a silver plate in the bottom. Katherine remembered how remarkable the tomb had been to look upon because of the exquisite craftsmanship of both the coffin and the silver.

She opened the right door and shone her light along the floor to locate the hole that had remained from that day. Finding its near edge, she stepped up to it, leaned over, and pointed her flashlight into the shaft. A blinding reflection bounced back. She angled her light to the side so she could get a better look at the tomb.

## THE POSSESSION OF BLACKSTONE MANSION

There it was. The empty concrete coffin lay at the bottom with its back plate of pure, polished, mirror-like silver. *What is going on here?* Though she was no expert on burial rituals, especially not any eccentric ones of the ruling class, she couldn't imagine why the Blackstones had covered up Eileen's murder in this way. "And why was she moved from the cemetery?" If they had only wanted to hide her body, they could have just left her in Silas's grave. No one would have ever come looking there. But they not only buried her there, they then removed her and constructed this elaborate tomb. "At such expense." Katherine was guessing, even at the level of inflation at the time, it would have cost thousands if not tens of thousands to build it. "Doesn't make any sense. There must've been a reason."

She scanned what little of the tomb she could see in a crisscross pattern. She didn't expect to discover anything more illuminating, but figured she might as well take as thorough a look as she could before leaving it be.

Sparkling. By the foot of the coffin. She pointed her beam. Two side-by-side twinkles.

She paused and dropped her flashlight, letting it dangle from her wrist. She crouched next to the hole and began the slow descent down its side. It was easy going. The dug-out masonry had left a craggy wall with lots of hand-holds. She was a little scared, though, that the distance she'd have to drop from the bottom of the hole to the tomb's floor was higher than it looked from the surface.

After several seconds, she felt air beneath her feet. *Careful, Kat. Don't wanna break your back on the coffin's edge.* She fumbled with her flashlight.

The tomb filled with light again, much of it reflecting off the coffin's silver plate. She saw that the drop to the bottom was a few feet, but not too far.

She let go. *Bam!* She hit the floor. The distance had been high enough that she felt a sting in the soles of her feet and in her toes. She forgot about the pain, though, as she shone her light around the tomb.

The cylindrical wall was built from the same style of masonry as the layer between the tomb and the surface. She pointed her flashlight at the coffin's foot. Two silver stripes embedded in the floor. They looked like the lines that connected components in... "Circuits." Yes, it looked like the coffin was one major piece of a computer's motherboard, that these stripes led it to some other.

She followed them to the wall, where they disappeared into the stone. "Oh my God. If these connector things go in, that means... Was this tomb even built to hide Eileen? Or was it *always* here?"

She traced her beam along the wall, not sure what she was looking for. "If it was always here..." She kept searching, though still wasn't seeing anything that stuck out to her.

*There.* She saw that where her flashlight's light was hitting the wall, it cast shadows at sharp angles. She walked closer and saw what was going on. Her light was revealing the edge of a circular staircase built directly into the wall. It started from the coffin's right side, continued around its head, and past its left side.

She walked around to the coffin's right side. She started up the stairs, half expecting some booby trap to spring on her. She continued up as far as she could go. Featureless stone walls on all three sides. "Only meant to be opened from the other side?" She returned to the coffin. She looked up at the hole's wall. "Okay, how am I gonna get outta here?"

She scanned the wall with her flashlight. There were plenty of clear hand-holds. She stepped on top of the coffin's edge, and let her flashlight dangle from her wrist as she reached for the hole's wall. While she could get an easy grip, it was soon clear that she didn't have the upper-body strength to lift herself out.

She sighed. "Well, this is embarrassing." She unclipped her walkie-talkie. She turned it on and pressed the call button. "Uh, guys? I seem to have fallen down a hole."

## 11

"I don't understand what you were doin' down there," Shane said, as he and Kirk finished helping Katherine out of the west tower's floor hole.

"Call it curiosity." Katherine didn't want to get into it with Shane, not only because he tended to be on the ornery side, but also because she just didn't want to get into it.

"Well, you're right on time," Kirk said.

Katherine regarded him curiously.

"To collect lunch orders," Kirk said.

"Right. That. Everybody line up." Katherine took out her phone. The guys gathered around and she wrote it all down. "Got it. I'll be back in a little under an hour."

The guys thanked her, and she headed down the hallway toward the entryway.

"Kat? A minute?" Kirk asked.

"Yeah, walk me down the hill," Katherine said.

They walked in silence until they had almost reached the entryway.

He spoke up in a hushed tone. "What were you really doing down there?"

She checked behind them to make sure none of the guys had followed. Satisfied, she took Kirk's arm and leaned in. "It's like a whole temple in there!"

"Temple?"

"Not literally, but it's, like, there's the coffin and the silver-mirror thing…"

"Yeah?"

She put a finger to her lips. They were both silent as they walked through the entryway. Once outside and heading down the hill, she continued. "And there are these connectors, like on a circuit board, that branch out to who knows where else in the house?"

"Yeah, it's all pretty strange."

"I think they built Eileen's tomb for a purpose."

"Beyond her."

"Yeah, there's no way whoever built it did so just to hide her body."

"I don't understand, so they didn't intend to hide her there?"

"No, they did, just that they didn't build it specifically for that."

"So then, why put her there?"

"And why is it so elaborate? When we're done here today, I'm gonna do some digging."

"Sounds like a plan."

"Kat?" Luke called.

Katherine found him standing right outside the gate. He waved and gave Kirk a nod.

"Luke, what the hell?" Katherine exited the gate. "What are you doing here? I work here!" She got in his space. "I'm at work here!"

"You haven't answered my calls or texts," Luke said. "Did you get the flowers?"

"Yes, I—" She threw Kirk a glance. *Crap. Never told Kirk about them. Now he'll think I was hiding them.*

Kirk cocked a curious eyebrow, but said nothing.

*Yep. He definitely thinks I hid that.* She turned Luke away from Kirk. "I got the flowers and under any normal circumstance, I would've found the gesture very romantic, but one, we're broken up—"

"I never agreed to that," Luke said.

"Um, dude, you don't *have* to. Two, this is approaching stalking territory!" Katherine tried to keep her voice down, but failed.

"Everything okay?" Kirk asked her, but kept his eyes on Luke.

"All good, junior," Luke said with a condescending smile.

Kirk nodded, looking like he was fighting to stop himself from rushing over and tearing Luke's head off.

*I am right with you, Kirk.* "Yeah, it's fine. Luke was just leaving," she assured Kirk, though she didn't take her eyes off Luke. "How'd you even find me, anyway? You know what? I don't wanna know. Goodbye, Luke."

She turned back to the gate, intending to rejoin Kirk, then remembered that the whole reason they'd come down here was for her to go get lunch for the guys. She did an about-face and marched for her car.

"All I'm asking"—Luke said as he followed her—"is a chance to explain. No dinner. Not even lunch. Just coffee."

Kirk started to leisurely follow them. He walked through the gate. "Sounds to me like she's been pretty clear."

Luke looked back for an instant. "Yeah, thanks." He asked Katherine, "When did he graduate? Like, last year?"

She reached her car, unlocked the door, and faced him, fuming. "I don't see how that's any of your goddamn business!"

"You're right. I'm sorry. It's not. I'm sorry." He nodded at Kirk. "I'm sorry." He begged Katherine. "Please. Just coffee."

She stared off into the woods, then looked at Kirk. He gazed right back, but said nothing. She addressed Luke, pointing between him and herself. "*We* are not together. *We* are not getting back together." She pointed between Kirk and herself. "Because *we* are together, I hope, I want, whatever."

Luke threw Kirk a glance, then looked back at her. "I understand." He reiterated to Kirk. "I understand."

"Just coffee?" she asked.

Luke held up his hands in surrender. "Just coffee. So I can explain."

"Nothing else," she insisted.

"Nothing else."

"Then I guess I can text after I'm done here."

Luke nodded.

"Now, you need to go, leave me to my business, and Luke, you better not pull a stunt like this again. Seriously, dude. Boundaries."

Luke nodded as he backed away to his rental. "I will talk to you soon." He offered Kirk a parting salute. "You have a good day." He got into his car and drove off down the hill.

Katherine faced Kirk. "I'm sorry. I had no idea he was gonna do that."

Kirk nodded. "Go get lunch." He walked back through the gate.

"Yeah." She wanted to say, *Kirk, we're not together. Seriously. We're not. If it weren't so cold out here, I'd jump you right now in the middle of this road.* But by the expression on his cute face, she was pretty sure he wasn't in the mood, that he was most likely wrestling with what was going on between her and Luke. First there was Luke's showing up at her place, interrupting her date with Kirk. Then there were the flowers, which she so wished she'd at least mentioned. Now Luke was dropping by here. It probably looked like she was leaning toward getting back together.

And now that she had to get lunch for the team, so shouldn't hang around, it hardly seemed like the time to explain everything to Kirk. And that would be assuming he was even willing to listen.

"Kirk," she said in an attempt to smooth things over, even if only a little.

He didn't turn around. "See you soon, Kat." He headed up the hill without another word.

She faced her car door with a heavy sigh. She got in and headed to Blackstone.

---

Katherine picked up all the lunches from the diner and Blackstone's sole miniscule convenience store, and soon was back on the road to the mansion. The whole time, she was thinking about how best to get rid of Luke and wondering if accepting his invitation to coffee had even been a good idea. What was he going to say that he hadn't already said?

As she turned onto Promontory on the last leg to the mansion, she thought about the hole in the floor of its west tower, the concrete coffin, and the silver connectors. She felt a chill as if someone unseen had rolled down the rear driver's side window. She rubbed the back of her neck and checked the rearview.

Those terrible vacant eye sockets stared right back at her! It was the same skeletal visage she'd seen at the bowling alley.

She shouted and simultaneously swerved to her left and hit the gas.

His jaw cracked as his guttural groan filled her ears. And that stench! That awful stench!

Before she knew what was happening, she saw tree trunks flying straight at her. "No!" At the last second, before she plowed head-on into one, she jacked the steering wheel to the right and slammed the brakes.

The maneuver didn't stop her from hitting the tree, but it did stop her from crushing herself into it. *Bam!* The car hit the tree squarely in the rear driver's side. The window exploded. Branches stabbed into the back seat.

Silence.

She sat there for a full minute. She heard no more ghostly voices, so lifted her eyes to the rearview.

The specter was gone.

The sacks of lunches had spilled all over, and many were now covered in piles of branches and leaves. *Wonder if any of those are salvageable.*

She waited another minute for the ghost to reappear, but he didn't. She attempted to open her door, but it didn't budge. She reached over to the passenger's side and unlocked it. She climbed over the gear-shift, opened the door, and slid out.

She turned around and assessed the damage. It didn't look like the car was totaled, but it would require work, lots of work, with the entire rear left quarter completely smashed in.

She sighed. *How am I gonna explain destroying their lunch? Guess I'd better call. First Kirk, then AAA.* She unclipped her walkie-talkie and clicked it on. "Hey, Kirk? Got a little sitch."

---

Katherine and Kirk stood by the side of the road as a slender AAA driver with a bushy gray mustache finished hooking her car up to his truck.

"The exact same, uh, guy?" Kirk asked.

She nodded. "Plain as day."

"Kat, this is bad."

"Really?"

"No, I'm serious."

"So am I."

"It's one thing to see something in the tower attic."

"Something?"

"It's another at King's Lanes, but in your car? On the road?"

"You don't think I saw him."

"I'm sure you saw *something*."

"Or her? You don't think I saw Eileen."

"Kat, I didn't say that."

"You didn't have to. I heard it in your voice."

He faced her. "Look, I don't know what to think. It all sounded plausible when you found that body and predicted the murder weapon and all that, but this is different."

"How?"

"I... I dunno. It just feels different."

"Maybe they're related."

"So, they murdered Eileen in the same house as some guy?"

"Why not? Murder seemed to be the Blackstones' favorite hobby."

"I dunno what to tell you."

"What about the pendant?"

"The what?"

She practically tore open her purse and yanked out the black-and-platinum pendant. She held it up and shook it, nearly in his face. "This!"

"Okay?"

"The second ghost didn't appear until *after* I found this."

"So what's that mean?"

"I dunno, but there must be a way to find out."

"What are you gonna do?"

She started for the AAA truck. "Hitch a ride back."

"We're not done here." He pointed in the mansion's direction.

"You're their supervisor. Supervise. Make sure they safely move everything into my space."

"I can't."

She stopped and faced him. "Why not?"

"I don't have any keys."

She felt embarrassed, defeated, and ashamed. Her face fell. She shook her head. She marched back to him, reached into her purse, and took out a set of keys. "Here." She held them out to him.

He accepted the keys. "I'll bring 'em by later."

She was already on her way to the AAA truck. "See you then. And sorry about the lunches!"

He waved. "No problem. We'll get more."

She greeted the driver. "How's your day going?"

"Can't complain. What's that you got there?" He pointed to the pendant.

"Goth jewelry." She shoved it back into her purse.

## 12

The AAA driver dropped Katherine off at her building. They exchanged information so she could pick up her car later. Much later, it sounded like, as the damage to where it had hit that tree was pretty extensive. He assured her someone would contact her once her car was ready.

*Means I'm probably gonna have to hitch a ride with Kirk until further notice*, she thought as she entered the complex. She was already dreading the next time she spoke to him, which would be tonight after he and his team were done dropping off the mansion's pieces at her store. With everything from her having failed to mention the flowers Luke had sent to Kirk's having witnessed her agreeing to meet Luke for coffee later, it all spelled nothing but awkwardness between her and Kirk.

She couldn't worry about that now. *Guess I'd better text Luke. Get this over with*, she thought as she set her purse on the sofa. Thinking on the pendant, she

# THE POSSESSION OF BLACKSTONE MANSION

asked the living room, "You gonna jump out at me here too, Vern?"

The room was quiet.

"Hope not, 'cause you already totaled my car."

The room remained silent.

Not satisfied, she went into the bathroom. Feeling an anticipatory jolt of adrenaline, she braved gazing into the mirror.

Nothing but her reflection.

She threw back the shower curtain. The tub was empty.

She stuck her head in the bedroom. It was also void of ghosts. She peeled back the bed's covers. Nothing but an empty mattress underneath.

She stood up straight and sighed with annoyance. "So do you just pop out when it's most likely to wrap me around a friggin' tree?" She waited a few seconds, as if Vernon's ghost might suddenly appear and answer her question. She rubbed the back of her neck, then shook her head. "Regular old room temp."

She returned to the living room, took off her jacket, and dropped it next to her purse. She sat, then pulled out the pendant, stroking the platinum vein for a long minute.

She set the piece on the coffee table and took out her phone. She sat back into the sofa and texted Luke.

> Done for the day. Let's

She really wanted to say "get this over with," but she decided not to be rude. As much as she wanted him to understand that they were done, she had to admit that there was a certain charm in his actions. She couldn't deny that he did care.

> Let's meet.

*Short and sweet.*
He responded immediately.

> Absolutely. Where?

She thought of suggesting some Starbucks somewhere, but selfishly decided on Blackstone's diner. Having Wendy there would boost her confidence.

> There's a diner in Blackstone. Only one. Great hot cocoa.

A lie. The hot cocoa was barely potable, but she felt like she needed to rationalize the choice.

> Sounds good. Address?

She sent it.

> See you there in 20?

> You're that close?

> Yep.

# THE POSSESSION OF BLACKSTONE MANSION

> See you there.

The second she sent the text, she remembered she didn't have a car and Kirk, her usual ride, was still occupied with the mansion. That and she hardly would have expected her would-be boyfriend to drop her off at a parting date with her ex. She hoped Uber operated all the way out here in the outskirts of Blackstone.

According to her phone, it did. She ordered her ride and went outside to wait. The app's indicator said ten minutes, then updated to seven, then eight, then ten again. Ironically, by the time it showed, it looked like the wait time plus the ride would end up taking almost as long as it would have for her simply to have walked. Well, maybe not quite that long, but that's how it seemed.

Upon strapping in, she suspiciously eyed the rearview. *If Vern decides to show up, at least we won't crash.*

She did not remove her eyes from that mirror the whole way.

---

Katherine stepped confidently up to the diner's door. Whereas in her first days in Blackstone, she'd found its bell really irritating, she now derived a certain comfort from its *clang clang* as she swung the door open.

She entered and took a quick look around. There were three customers on the left side, empty seats in the middle, and—*What?* Luke was already there, already sipping on coffee, which meant he'd been there for probably at least ten minutes.

*How did he beat me?* She concluded he must have been hanging out in the immediate area waiting for her call, not twenty minutes away, as he'd claimed.

Wendy waved and greeted her. "'Afternoon, hon. This your gentleman caller?" She threw Luke a glance and Katherine a coy grin.

*Yeah, yeah, Wendy. He's handsome, but that's not all that matters. Hey, maybe I can pawn him off on her. Bet he could keep her entertained for at least a few nights.* "'Gentleman caller.' Like that." She sat next to Luke.

Wendy was ready to take her order. "What can I get you?"

"Just hot cocoa," Katherine said.

"Comin' right up." Wendy winked.

*Stop it, Wendy!* "You beat me," she told Luke as she set her purse aside and took off her jacket.

He shrugged. "Eh, was in the area."

"What are you always doing 'in the area'?"

"Trying to connect with you."

"Yeah, that's called stalking, Luke."

"Not with your girlfriend."

"We're not together. I thought I made that abundantly clear."

"You never said anything."

"Um, I thought my taking off with all my stuff and not one word was pretty damn clear."

Wendy set Katherine's cocoa in front of her.

"Thanks, Wendy," Katherine said.

Wendy nodded, threw Luke another glance, grinned, and walked away.

*Take him, please!*

"It was one fight, Kat," Luke said.

Katherine turned to face him and looked him dead in the eyes. "It was *not* one fight! It was one fight in which you started it by saying, 'Quit your whining'! Who does that, Luke?"

He looked away.

"Look at me," she said.

He obeyed.

"Who does that?" she asked again.

"Katherine, I am *so* sorry. I didn't mean to be so insensitive. I just... it'd been nonstop."

"There you go again! Nonstop? Are you kidding me?"

"I'm sorry. I didn't mean 'nonstop—'"

"Dean was my best friend!" Her tone was loud enough that the other customers took notice. She didn't give a damn.

"I know."

"Best friend, Luke!"

"I know."

"Like, my whole friggin' life!"

"I know. I'm sorry."

"And you called it 'incessant whining'!"

"Kat, how can I make it up to you?"

"You just don't get it."

"Then explain it to me."

"It wasn't that it was a fight. It wasn't just that it was about Dean. It was... Ryan threatened to *sue* me. Sue me!"

"He was never gonna... I would've gotten him to settle for nothing."

"Everyone cut me off! Everyone!"

"I was just as angry about that as you were."

"And then you, my boyfriend, my partner. If things had gone better, who knows? Maybe more! You say 'incessant whining'!"

"Kat, tell me what I can do."

"I had lost everyone and what I needed was someone. Someone to be there for me when it gets tough. And ultimately, you saw me as a frickin' inconvenience."

"That's not true!"

She took several swallows from her hot cocoa, then stood up. "Luke, I came here as a courtesy because you're a generally decent guy. But I'm gonna be brutally honest with you."

"Please."

"We weren't working. I knew it. I think you knew it. Fact was, the fight sped up the process. I'd been thinking for weeks of leaving you. Dean's death and funeral put a pause on it, but it was gonna happen."

"I see." His tone told her that he had truly no idea.

"I don't love you. I'm not going to. I don't think you love me either."

He didn't challenge her assessment.

"Now please, live your life," she said. "Your flying out here, the flowers, they were nice gestures, but now it's time to let me live mine."

"Is it the five-year-old?"

She sighed hard. "Not that it's *any* of your goddamn business, but yeah, Kirk is part of it. I'm hoping we have something. He's already shown me so much more consideration than you ever did."

Luke nodded.

"Hey." She waited for him to raise his eyes to hers. "We good? You gonna stop showing up at my work, sending flowers, and all that?"

He nodded.

She took out her wallet.

"No, I've got it," he said.

"I don't wanna owe you anything."

"Kat, come on." He took out his wallet.

She beat him to it, slapping a twenty on the counter and downing the rest of her cocoa. Putting her wallet back, she finished with, "Have a good flight back and please, Luke"—she gave him a stern look—"seriously, have a good life."

He nodded and sipped his coffee.

She exited the diner and heaved an intensely relieved sigh. *Thank God that's over with! Now I can get back to Kirk. If he'll have me. If not, guess I can google the nearest convent.* Lacking a car or an AAA driver to give her a ride, she ordered another Uber back to her apartment. The only thing left to do today was to get her keys from Kirk.

---

Katherine glared at her laptop's screen. It displayed ninety million open browser tabs. One huge batch had to do with her search for more information on the mansion's floor plan. The farthest she'd gotten was a county site that had a number for a records department she'd have to call during the week.

Another batch of tabs was text and image searches on the pendant's symbol. For the latter, she'd uploaded the picture she'd sent Miles to show his guy Nigel.

Nothing had come up.

At least, nothing obvious. She found lots of pages with similar symbols, many of them referring to death metal album covers, fantasy role-playing video games, some to alchemy, and some to the mysticism of various religions, but never that specific symbol.

"How is that even possible?" she asked her laptop's screen. "Is it so unique that it escaped Google's clutches?"

A third search category, only one tab, was on Vernon Blackstone. He'd died in 1922, a year after his son, Reginald. From all accounts, Vernon's death seemed to have been from natural causes.

*Then why the hell is he haunting me?*

In the middle of scanning down the latest crop of images that didn't resemble the pendant, but the act of which at least made her feel like she was doing something, her buzzer rang.

She got up, ran into the living room, and checked the monitor. It was Kirk. She buzzed him in. She then stood by the door to be ready to open it in what she hoped would be a bit of a sexy manner. *Slowly? How am I gonna make this sexy?*

A minute later, she heard footsteps approach. Then there was a very matter-of-fact sounding three strikes on the door. She frowned. *Sounds like he's only here to drop off the keys.* She opened the door.

Kirk stood there with a pleasant, if not entirely happy, expression on his face. "'Evening."

"'Evening. How'd it go?"

"Fine. Everything's in your store, safe and sound."
"Great. Thanks."
He nodded.

"Um, won't you come in?" She realized she'd forgotten to open the door in a slow, sexy way, so now she felt embarrassed and awkward even though he wasn't aware of her intentions.

"I think I should just..." He reached into his pocket, took out her keys, and held them out.

She accepted them. "Sure you don't wanna...?" She opened the door wider and gestured for him to enter.

He sighed. "Look, Kat, I don't know what's goin' on with you and Luke."

"Nothing. Absolutely nothing."

"Then why didn't you tell me about the flowers?"

"I honestly didn't think of it. They rotted so quickly."

"Rotted?"

"It's... Don't worry about it."

"And you didn't have coffee with him?"

"I did, but *only* to be explicit with him that it was over."

"So, it wasn't over before?"

"For me, of course it was, but not quite for him."

"You told me he dumped you."

*Goddamn it, Kat!* "Yes. I did say that." And now she had no idea what else to say that wouldn't make this so much worse. "Come on, Kirk. Just come in."

"Kat..." He stood his ground.

"I said he dumped me because it was an economy of language. Easier to say than, 'I took off without a word after a fight, with all my crap packed, and told him nothing.'"

"That's what you did?"

"I'm not proud of it, but Luke and I, it wasn't working, it wasn't gonna work, and the whole mess around Dean's death had made it so much worse."

"You could've told me it wasn't working, that you left."

"Yes, I could've. I guess, honestly, I guess I wanted you to feel sorry for me and having been dumped lends itself to that."

"It's just, Katherine..." He searched for how to continue his sentence.

She grinned a little out of frustration. "I hate it when you're formal with me."

"You've so far had a bit of a loose relationship with the truth."

"And each time, I had a pretty good reason." Her tone sounded so much more defensive than she intended.

This wasn't going well.

"Look, you free Friday, Saturday?" she asked.

"I dunno. I might be. Let's keep talking."

*Phew! At least there's hope.* "I can do talking."

He grinned. "Okay. Good night, Kat. See you tomorrow."

"'Night, Kirk. See you then." She closed the door and retreated to her bedroom, where she spent another hour leaping down rabbit holes she hoped would give her more information on the pendant's symbol, but none of which bore fruit.

Her phone *buzzed*. She didn't recognize the number, but it wasn't in the States. "Hello?"

"Hello, is this Katherine Norrington?" a very nasal, very impatient male voice asked.

"Speaking." She stood and paced.

"Good evening, Ms. Norrington, or at least I think it is on your side of the pond."

"It is. And Kat, please."

"I'm sorry?"

"You can call me Kat, short for Katherine." *Probably wasn't necessary to explain how nicknames work.*

"Hm, 'Kat,' yes. Very well, Kat, this is Nigel Hargrove, Miles's acquaintance."

"Yes, of course! Thanks for calling, Nigel."

"Yes, so Miles showed me your symbol."

*Is he gonna drag this whole thing out?* "Great. So, what do you think?"

"Where did you find this?"

*God, what do I tell him? If I say 'secret chamber,' he'll think I'm crazier than Kirk does. But I can't just say 'on the floor,' can I?* "I found it at this mansion out here."

"Interesting." He didn't sound like he was going to say anything else.

"Interesting?"

"Yes."

She didn't want to sound rude, but this was already such a slow, awkward conversation that she wanted to speed it up. "How so?"

He heaved a little sigh. She wasn't sure whether it was her or the subject that was frustrating him. She hoped for the latter.

"How much do you know about the occult, Ms. Norrington?" he asked.

"'Kat,' please."

"Kat, sorry."

"The occult?"

"Yes, witchcraft, secret societies, all that."

"Yes, I know what the occult is, but no, I have to admit my knowledge is lacking, at least outside of how it interacts with antiques."

"Ah, that's right. Your expertise, like Miles's, is in antiques."

"Exactly."

"Well, Kat"—each time he said her name, it sounded like he was trying to put on an ill-fitting pair of boots—"the image you sent is of an ancient occult symbol."

"It is?"

"Yes. The history isn't clear. Some say it dates back to early Middle Eastern civilizations, some to early Far Eastern, some say it has no history at all."

"I don't understand."

"Well, there are very fringe voices who say that the symbol originates not of this world."

"You mean aliens?"

He sounded a little frustrated at her conclusion. "No. A realm beyond our reality."

She spoke the word in awe, "Beyond."

"Yes. In fact, I've only ever seen one other example of this symbol. It was inscribed on an ancient parchment discovered in a chest which itself had been buried for centuries in a dwelling in Iran."

"Iran?"

"Yes."

"So, Nigel, in your expert opinion, what does this all mean?"

"In my expert opinion?"

"Yes."

He drew in a deep breath as if about to pronounce something mind-blowingly profound. "I don't know."

"What do you mean, you don't know?"

"I mean, I don't know."

"I don't understand."

"Which portion of my previous sentence would you like me to elaborate on?"

"No, I don't mean I don't understand what you meant by 'I don't know.' I mean, I don't understand this whole thing. Why this symbol was at the mansion, what its relationship to the mansion is, why the only other example was found in some ancient basement in Iran."

He sounded confused. "I never said it was found in a basement."

"No, I know, I was suggesting, extrapolating."

"Ah. I see."

"So there's nothing else you can tell me about the symbol?"

"I'm afraid very little."

"Go on."

"In many occult and alchemical symbols, there's a tendency toward representing the cosmos and man's relationship to it."

"All right."

"There is also a tendency toward representing man's desire to harness or manipulate that relationship."

"I'm with you."

"While I don't know, I conjecture that with your symbol, the central equilateral triangle likely represents the cosmos. The great balance of things."

"Okay."

"The, uh, bottom triangle, the one that looks rather like a V?"

"Yes?"

"It seems plausible that it represents some sort of means of manipulation, as I'd suggested, of the balance of that cosmos. Perhaps a door or a key of some kind."

"A key."

"Yes. Now keep in mind, I don't actually know. I'm merely speculating based on years of research into these sorts of things and patterns that have emerged from them."

"I understand."

He paused a good long time.

"Nigel?" she asked.

He took a breath. "A word of caution, Ms. Norrington—Kat?"

"Of course."

"I don't mean to alarm you and I'm not a superstitious man myself, but I posit that there is a reason that this symbol is so unbelievably rare and that you found it in your mansion."

"Are you saying there's a relationship between the two?"

"I'm saying that where there is smoke, there is often fire. Some fires you do *not* want to play with."

"No. Of course not." Her mind swam with the myriad possibilities of what he was saying implied.

"Well, then, if that's all…"

"Yeah," she said, still distracted.

"I bid thee adieu."

It occurred to her that he was about to hang up. "Nigel, wait!"

"Yes?" He sounded like he was seriously losing his patience.

"Can I call you again? If I find out more, have any more questions?"

He hesitated for what felt like a solid fifteen seconds. "If absolutely necessary."

"I promise, if I were to reach out for anything further, it wouldn't be trivial."

"Very well, then." He next sounded like he was reading from a barely rehearsed script. "If you have any further questions or need further clarification, then don't hesitate to ring." By the end of his sentence, he sounded very relieved.

"Wonderful. Thank you."

"Good evening, Kat." He hung up.

*A friggin' occult symbol? What the hell is going on at Blackstone mansion?*

## 13

*Buzz! Buzz!* The sound brutally invaded the sleep Katherine had struggled so hard to attain. Ever since her first encounter with Vernon's ghost, but especially since her second, which had led directly to her crashing into a tree, the very notion of getting solid, restful sleep was becoming harder and harder to even fathom.

*Buzz!* She rolled over in bed and reached out to her nightstand. Her fingers touched the blasted vibrating device, but the second she attempted to lift it, it dropped to the floor. "Damn it!"

She sat up and half rolled, half scooted over to the edge of the bed, taking most of the covers with her. She nearly fell out trying to grab her still-*buzzing* phone. She finally extricated her legs from underneath the covers and swung them over the side of the bed. She reached down and picked up her phone.

It stopped buzzing. She checked the ID. Jordan. And the time said 6:00. She groaned. As she was about to tap his number to call back, her phone started *buzzing* all over again. She answered. "Jordan?"

"Hey! Kat! 'Morning! I wake you?" Jordan sounded very strange. Not only manic. He sounded the kind of manic one put on to mask something else, something much more disturbed.

"It's 6:00!"

"Hey, yeah! Six is in the morning."

"Yeah, Jordan, I wasn't questioning your assessment of the time of day. I was complaining about the fact that you're calling me at 6:00 on a Sunday."

"Oh, I'm sorry that your *employer* is calling you about issues that concern your *employment* on a Sunday. Aren't you and the crew working today, anyway?"

"Yeah, but not for another couple of hours!"

"Then consider this extra breakfast-getting time."

"Are you okay, Jordan?"

"What? Yes! Of course! Totally okay! My okay-ness is off the charts! So very, very okay." His tone shifted to deep concern. "Why, do I not sound okay?"

"No, um... No, no. It's fine. What did you need?"

His concerned tone lingered. "Why do you ask?"

"Your call, Jordan! Why did you call? At 6:00?"

His tone fired straight back up to manic. "Oh! Right! That! Yes, of course! Why did I call? Oh right.

I just wanted to let you know that you're meeting with the electrician Tuesday morning."

"Great."

"Exactly. Gotta get that power flowing."

"I mean, okay, but we've actually been doing fine without it. I understand that equipment rental is a pain, but I'm guessing so will be wiring everything."

"I want the mansion ready for Halloween."

"What?"

"It's a primarily children's holiday celebrating the macabre."

"I know what Halloween is!"

"Oh, I was about to say, weird you hadn't heard of it."

"No, I asked 'what' because I don't understand how you think that's possible. Halloween's, like, less than a week away."

"So?"

"Jordan, if you want electricity, it's gonna take at least a few days alone to set that up. If you also want the mansion cleared out of antiques, that's gonna take a few weeks, and that's not including cleaning the place, let alone the days on which the crew has other jobs."

"So hire crew that *doesn't* have other jobs."

She desperately wanted to reach through the phone and strangle him. "Also, depending on how you wanna use the mansion for Halloween, that'll take setup as well."

"Oh, that won't be a problem," he said with supreme confidence, as if he had a fully formed plan tucked up his sleeve.

"I'm sorry? How so?"

"I'm gonna spin."

She assumed he meant as in records as in he'd DJ in the mansion, but she wanted to make sure. "You mean you're gonna DJ an event?"

"Exactly. It'll be the grand re-opening of Blackstone mansion on Halloween night."

"So you're just gonna set up a generator and lights in the entryway and, uh, that's it?"

"No, Kat. You and the electrician are gonna figure out the electricity situation. The electric company is then gonna handle the light, power, whatever. I will then host the biggest Halloween blowout the Pacific Northwest has ever seen."

Her head was swimming with questions, concerns, and incredulity over what he wanted to do. "Let me see if I'm getting all this. You're gonna host a party."

"Yes."

"At the mansion?"

"Yes."

"Will there be drinks, food?"

"Yes."

"I assume catered?"

"Yes."

"And will there be anything else going on?"

"Such as?"

"I mean, most modern Halloween activity involves a haunted house maze."

"Excellent idea, Kat!"

"No, Jordan, I—"

"I never would've thought of that! A haunted house maze in an actual haunted house! I mean, not really, but you know what I mean."

*You have no idea. Wait. Vernon showed up outta the frickin' blue during my date with Kirk. And that was at some random bowling alley! What's he gonna do during a rager at his own house?* She couldn't think of a way to ask that, so she asked something else that she hoped would deter Jordan. "How are you gonna host a maze in a house mostly full of priceless antiques?"

"Rope it off."

"And who's designing this maze?"

"If I can't find anyone else, I'll do it."

*What?*

"I can base it off of the actual murder that took place there." He was referring to the murder, burial, and reburial of Eileen Byrne, his many times great aunt, who, though he was unaware, had until recently literally been haunting the place ever since. She and likely many others.

"And how are you getting the word out so all the kids know to drive all the way out here on Halloween night?"

"Hire a PR company."

"Look, Jordan, I told you, I'm not an event planner, so the best I can do is the job we agreed on as quickly as possible. Beyond that..."

"I understand, Kat. You do your thing, I'll do mine."

"So am I moving everything out faster, or..."

"Do what you think is best. Use your judgment. I'll figure out everything else on my end."

*Unlikely, given you can't even be bothered to handle your own house's electricity.* "I will take your lead."

"I knew I could count on you, Kat. Call me with any updates."

"Will do. Bye." She hung up.

She set her phone back on the nightstand, stood, stretched, and went to her drawers to grab some clothes. She took a quick shower, got dressed, and threw together some breakfast.

At 7:30, Kirk did not buzz. He did not call. He texted simply...

> Here

She let out a pathetic sigh. *Great, we're not even, like, really dating and I'm in the dog house.* She threw on her jacket, grabbed her purse, and ran down to meet him.

Getting in his truck, she put on the brightest smile she could muster. "Hi! 'Morning!"

He gave her a quick, polite nod and a little grin. "'Morning."

"Ready for the rigors of the day?"

"Yep." He got them going.

They'd only driven a block when she requested, "Can you pull over just one sec?"

He obeyed without a word. They sat by the side of the road.

"Are you mad at me?" she asked.

He shook his head. "Nope."

"Well, what's going on?"

"Nothing."

"You didn't call when you arrived."

"Figured I wouldn't waste the time."

"You didn't even get out of your truck."

"Knew you were gonna get in."

"Kirk, come on."

Now it was his turn to heave a heavy sigh. "Katherine, everything was great until after our dinner, when Luke showed up."

"I didn't know he was gonna do that."

"And then he sent flowers."

"Didn't know he was gonna do that either."

"Which you didn't tell me about."

"I forgot about it. I swear."

"Then he shows up at the mansion."

"Again, I didn't know he was gonna do that."

"Then you have coffee with him."

"Only to..." she trailed off. He was making his point.

"It's just... for a relationship that's over, it sure doesn't look like it. Which, honestly, is fine. None of my business. But that's how it looks."

"I understand how it *could have* looked that way, but I swear it's over."

"No more unannounced visits?"

"No."

"Random bouquets?"

"None."

"No more coffee dates?"

"Had you seen us on that"—she held up quote fingers—"'date,' you would've seen it wasn't a date."

He smiled genuinely this time. "Okay." He got them going again.

After a few brief minutes of silence, she told him all about her call with Nigel. All about the mysterious nature of the pendant's symbol.

"So, what do you think?" Kirk asked.

"I mean, I don't know, but while you guys are at it today, I'm gonna take a look around."

"Be careful. Never know what might be lurking in those shadows."

## AUGUSTINE PIERCE

*Couldn't be worse than what was lurking in my rearview.* "I have a feeling I'll be fine."

They arrived at the mansion's gate and greeted the other guys. They all headed up the hill together. She directed them to the smoking room, one door past the music room, and before she knew it, the crew was hard at work under blazing lights like a well-oiled machine. They marched out tables, sofas, ashtray stands, and humidors like an army of worker ants.

After a minute of watching them work—it wasn't so bad seeing Kirk flex his muscles lifting his end of sofas—Katherine approached the bottom of the entryway staircase. The light from the right hallway spilled over the staircase's steps enough that she didn't need her flashlight to see them. She hiked to the second floor. There, a few inches above her head, she saw the plaque that hung on the corner of the two hallways that met there. Its triangular symbol gleamed in the hallway's light.

She took out the pendant and held it up to cover her view of the plaque's symbol. The bottom of the pendant—the V with the circle at its point—stuck out over the symbol. "All right, the plaque has no V." She threw a glance down the left hallway that connected with the west-east one. "The west tower."

She was about to set off when she paused. "Is Vern gonna terrorize me in here?" Considering the question, she realized that strangely enough, he hadn't contacted her at all while she'd been in the mansion. Only outside. Did that mean he couldn't or wouldn't?

She leaned over the right side of the staircase, focusing on the light spilling out from where Kirk and his crew were hard at work. *I guess if Vern shows up, or anyone else, the guys are within shouting distance.*

Feeling a little reassured, she turned on her flashlight, went down to the west-east hallway, and on to the west tower.

She opened its right door. It was so strange having entered so many times under so many conditions. The first to investigate the light in its attic. The second to follow the rotting-corpse manifestation of Eileen's ghost. The third to explore the tomb below the floor that Katherine and Kirk's crew had discovered on busting the floor wide open. Now she merely wanted to check the symbol that hung on the first floor's wall opposite its doors.

She ran down the stairs. She walked around the hole, being very careful not to misstep and fall in. Reaching the other side, she checked behind where she stood to make sure that were she to lean back while comparing the pendant with the wall's symbol, that she'd have plenty of room so she wouldn't fall in.

She pointed her flashlight at the wall's symbol. She held the pendant up between the symbol and her light.

The beam cast a shadow of the part of the pendant's symbol that was missing from the wall's version. The triangle's left point and its attached circle. She stepped away from the wall's symbol and retreated to the tower's doors. "Entryway's missing the bottom. West tower's missing the left. That means..."

She exited into the west-east hallway, but turned up the one that ran all the way to the north tower. She stopped at the tower's double doors. "If I'm right, there's gonna be another symbol in here." She shoved them open.

Firmly gripping her flashlight, she shone it straight ahead. Book spines strung with cobwebs. That was all she saw. *Right. It's another library, so I'm not gonna just see a symbol sticking out.* She walked over to the bookshelves against the flat wall. *I wonder...* She began carefully removing books, setting them on the seat of a nearby sofa. With four out of the way, she checked the wall.

Nothing.

"Maybe it's not literally at my eye level. Whoever built all this was probably taller." She moved five books from the shelf above.

More blank wall.

# THE POSSESSION OF BLACKSTONE MANSION

With a frustrated exhale, she stood back. "It's gotta be here." She scanned the room with her flashlight all over again. She paused when the beam skirted over the left corner where the sliding bookshelf met the semicircular part of the wall. "Right! The private study!"

She pulled the lever and eased the bookshelf-door open. Inside, she aimed her light at the middle of the study's semicircular wall, at the bookcase where she'd located the safe's keys. "Before I go digging in more bookcases..."

She lifted the flashlight to point directly above, just short of the ceiling.

*Boo-ya!*

There it was, mounted to a plaque just like the symbol in the entryway hall. This one wasn't the complete version of the pendant either. It had two small, twin equilateral triangles pointing up. They were connected via a third between them, pointed down. The third, down-pointing triangle was the V from the bottom of the other symbols. So the only difference between this symbol and the one from the pendant was that this one was missing its top point and attached circle. "Each tower is a portion of the symbol?"

She quickly retreated into the hallway and continued down to the east tower. She burst in to find a twin copy of the west tower with its own spiral staircase and floor boards. And exactly like the west one, this one had a symbol on the wall opposite the doors.

The symbol followed the same pattern as the others she'd seen. This time, its main triangle was missing its right point and attached circle. "Four for four."

She continued down the west-east hallway. She soon ran into Kirk's crew, so turned off her flashlight. She did her best to stay out of their way as she followed them into the entryway hall.

She stopped in the middle of the floor, the point where only weeks ago, Eileen Byrne's ghost had left her prized bronze cake stand, which Katherine then ultimately used to track down Eileen's remains.

Katherine held the pendant up to approximately where the entryway's symbol hung, beyond the top of the staircase. Using the light from the right doorway, she traced her finger along the pendant's lines. "If this is the entryway hall..." She touched the circle at the V's point at the bottom of the pendant. "And this is the north tower..." She tapped the circle attached to the uppermost point on the top of the pendant. "I can't believe I never noticed it before. That's why all the long hallways at all the weird angles. The four towers. This pendant—this symbol—*this* is the floor plan of Blackstone mansion."

## 14

"What you up to?" Kirk's voice hung with mild concern. He was standing a few feet to Katherine's right.

*What do I tell him? Well, he knows about my sightings of Eileen, and I guess Vernon. By comparison, this probably won't seem that crazy.* "Remember how I said reminiscing about encountering spirits was like just getting off the world's most intense roller coaster?"

"No."

"Well, it was. This? Like riding that same roller coaster backward. Come here." She grabbed his arm and dragged him out the front doors.

Outside, she closed the doors and looked around as if any of his team were about to show up.

"All good?" he asked.

"Yeah," she confirmed. She then showed him what she'd just discovered.

"Wow, can't believe I didn't notice it before."

"Right? We've only been in this place about a million times."

"So what's it mean?"

"The ghost who's contacted me twice, Vernon, both times he... growled at me. Very insistently."

"Maybe there are other bodies."

"Undoubtedly." That also hadn't crossed her mind.

"Maybe he wants you to stay away from them."

"I'm not sure about that. Why would one ghost care about my discovering other bodies? If others were murdered like Eileen, no one who's culpable would be alive today."

"So, then, why'd he growl at you?"

*I have no idea, Kirk.* "I'm gonna do some poking around."

"You sure that's a good idea? Last time you did that, you found a semi-mummified body."

"Yeah." She went back inside. "You guys keep going. I'm gonna..."

"Poke around?"

"Yeah."

With a nod, he rejoined the crew.

She turned on her flashlight. While the illumination from the doorway that led to the smoking room was enough that no one bumped into anything, it wasn't quite enough for her to feel like she was uncovering every nook and cranny. She started methodically scanning the floor and wall for any clues, from the right of the lit doorway all the way to the front doors.

She found nothing.

*I'm going about this all wrong, aren't I?* Retreating to the center of the hall, she walked through her thought process out loud, though not so loud that she'd alert Kirk and his crew. "I found Eileen's body buried in a specially built tomb. There were stairs walking up from it that had some exit that must've been accessible at some point. They didn't look built after the fact, after her burial."

She faced the door to the left of the staircase. Opening it, she hiked all the way to the west tower.

She opened the right door and pointed her light at the hole in the floor so she wouldn't fall in. "Since there are stairs coming up from down there"—she pointed at the hole as if she needed to remind it—"then there must be an entrance up here."

She walked the perimeter of the tower, always keeping a close eye on her feet so she didn't tumble into the hole.

Nothing.

She walked back to the doors and shone her light all over the room without focusing on any one thing in particular. "The Blackstones were eccentric, murderous conspirators, but that doesn't mean the house defies the laws of physics. Stairs went up from the tomb, so they must..."

She shone her light on the bottom steps of the spiral staircase. "Wait. I wonder if it's that obvious." She kept her light trained on the steps as she inched along the wall below the staircase's ascent. "Any space inside the wall has to be high enough for the average person to fit." She pressed her fingers to the cool stone as she continued. She stopped when she stood at a point where she thought there was enough room inside the wall for that average person.

She waved her light all over the area in front of her. At first, she found nothing unexpected. A plain flat stone wall. Then she saw it.

A seam.

Barely noticeable. She followed the line up to a little under six feet, where it pivoted ninety degrees to the left. She followed that horizontal line until it met a last line that returned to the floor.

*This is it!* She'd discovered what seemed like an entrance into the tomb below, a better entrance than dropping through the hole Shane had jackhammered. But the question remained. *How the hell do I get in?*

She stepped back from the rectangular outline. Now that she'd found it, under the illumination of her flashlight, it was as clear as could be that it had always been here. But just as obviously as the seam outlined the tomb's entrance, there was also no sign of how one entered it. There was no doorknob, no handle, nothing.

Watching her step, she returned to the tower's entrance and scanned the room all over again. *There has to be something obvious. If not a doorknob, then, well, something else.* She looked up and down the wall. The only thing that popped out was the tower's version of the pendant's symbol. *I mean, why not?* She walked around the hole and stood under the symbol. *Could it be?* She reached up and touched its V with the attached circle. The metal was colder than the stone. Braving that discomfort, she pressed her fingers into it.

It gave.

She could feel the metal move into the wall behind it. *Some kind of locking mechanism?* The movement halted. Whatever part she'd pushed had reached its end.

She shone her light around the room, but saw nothing changed, at least nothing obvious. The rectangular seam hadn't moved or opened.

She let go of the symbol. She heard its mechanism churn and snap back into place. The symbol now looked exactly as it always had.

She studied the symbol, its components. *A triangle, or mostly a triangle. A V. Circles. Those are the towers. The lines are the hallways. The missing left point means I'm in the west tower. Obviously. Pushing the thing into the wall didn't do anything, but the fact that I could push it, that must mean something.*

She pushed the symbol again. Metal ground against stone. *What if the nature of the symbol—missing the left point—is more than just orientation? More than just a map?* Following her hunch, she tried to keep the symbol pressed while also pushing it to the left, in the direction of the symbol's missing point.

It gave. The symbol moved smoothly, if not easily, to the left.

*Grind!* It was the sound of stone sliding against stone. It came from her right.

She turned to see what was happening, what had changed. To her delight, a rectangular slab, the one bound within the seam, receded into the wall.

*Oh my God. There it is.* Keeping her hand on the symbol, she lifted her flashlight to the discovered opening. Inside it, as far as her beam could reach, she found stairs going down. *The same ones I climbed that other day!* So it was true. The tomb contained beneath this tower had access to ground level. Given that this one's symbol granted such access, that meant that the others' symbols likely did as well. But what did that mean? *Are there bodies buried under each? If so, whose? The family's?*

She thought back to that book she'd found in the Blackstone wing of the Portland Art Museum, the one that had chronicled the history of the family's involvement in the museum. She remembered the fact that Gloria, the family's matriarch, had died only about a year after Eileen, Reginald a year after that, and as she'd learned recently, Vernon, a year after that.

*Since they buried Eileen here, and the others died in such quick succession... Could just be a coincidence, but... More symbols in the other towers. Does that mean they're all buried under the mansion? What about the family cemetery outside? Are all their graves empty?*

She released the metal symbol and felt it slide back into its initial position.

*Grind!* The wall's opening revealing the staircase that led down to the tomb sealed shut.

With these new possibilities of what the Blackstone family did with its dead swimming in her mind, she wandered out of the tower, through the west-east hallway, to the entryway. She stood there looking at the immense hall. She didn't even notice Kirk's crew was still hard at work. *I didn't see any entrance into any hidden passage. No rectangular seams in stone walls.*

She walked to the right side of the staircase, though was careful to stay out of the guys' way. She looked up the side. *Wonder if there's anything I missed here.* She circled around to the front and marched up the steps to the symbol on the plaque. She reached up and lay her hand on its triangle. *If the west tower's symbol moved to the left...* She pressed the metal. It gave way. She then felt the internal mechanism halt just as the west tower's had. *If all these symbols are more than maps...* She pushed the symbol down.

*Clack!* She heard wood slide against wood. The sound came from her right and straight down. *The staircase!* Without considering the mechanism of the switch she'd just released, she ran over to the side of the staircase and peered down.

Directly below her, a black rectangle of seemingly identical dimensions to the one she'd discovered in the west tower had opened in the staircase's side. She couldn't see much within it, but she swore she could see the top steps of descending stairs.

"Oh my God!" The second she uttered the words, the part of the staircase's side that had receded from the rectangular hole slid back into place, concealing any obvious sign of its existence.

"Kirk?" she asked, without considering whether he could even hear her.

---

"You sure this is safe?" Shane asked.

He and the rest of Kirk's crew had gathered around the place where Katherine had seen the right side of the entryway staircase open up. She'd excused them from work since she needed at least one additional set of hands, and likely would need more. She'd heard no objections.

Well, Kirk had paused for one second when she asked if everyone was okay with the work stoppage, but then he'd shrugged and muttered, "Jordan's dime."

"Completely," Katherine answered Shane. Her eyes were fixed on where the side of the staircase would recede once Kirk pressed the trigger—the symbol built into the plaque that hung only a few feet above them.

She wasn't sure. Not even a little. She was making a giant assumption based on the previously hidden spiral staircase embedded in the west tower wall. But this hall's hidden staircase? Assuming that what she'd seen only a few moments ago was that? She didn't know if it would lead down to a tomb like Eileen's or something far more sinister. Or maybe this was the entrance to a simple, everyday basement.

She wouldn't know until she'd ventured down.

"Everybody ready?" Kirk asked.

The rest of the group murmured its affirmation.

"Here goes!" Kirk pressed the symbol into the wall, then down.

*Scrape!* There was that exhilarating sound of wood dragging against wood that Katherine had so been anticipating since she'd rounded up the crew to check this out.

A rectangular section receded from the side of the staircase. In its place, there stood a solid black opening at the bottom right of which she could see stairs descending.

She turned on her flashlight and shone it toward the steps. The light revealed a staircase hidden away for who knew how long.

"Careful," Mac warned.

Katherine didn't look back at him or the rest of the crew, but nodded her acknowledgment. She stepped into the shadowy chamber.

"Kat? You good?" Kirk called from above.

"Yeah, just keep your hands on that symbol-switch," Katherine said.

"Hands aren't goin' anywhere."

Katherine turned onto the stone stairs, taking one at a time. After five, she suddenly wondered how many there were. She reminded herself that with this whole new experience, a possible new tomb lying beneath the entryway hall, she was making huge assumptions about its structure, layout, and contents.

After ten steps, she realized she could no longer hear any clear sign of the guys above. No chatter at all. While she knew she technically wasn't, she again felt completely alone.

She messed up her count of which step she was on. *Great*. Now she truly had no idea how far down she'd gone and, on the way back, would have no idea how far she'd have to go.

She heard a steady, repeating echo. It took her a full two seconds to realize it was the sound of her own footsteps bouncing off walls.

She'd reached the bottom, or nearly so. Two steps later, her flashlight revealed only solid ground. To make sure, she tapped her foot in front of her, but the result remained the same. No more steps.

Turning to her right, she faced the chamber. She lifted her light to scan the area. To her disappointment, she found no further symbols, writing, or any other sign that this room was anything other than, well, a room. It looked about double the size of the west tower's tomb, though not the full size of the entryway hall above. If she had to guess, it also looked like she was standing about double the depth as she had at the bottom of the other tomb.

Her light hit a horizontal line a few feet off the ground. There was a clear visual divide between the concrete below the line, which sat much closer to her, and the stone above it, which stood several feet away. The concrete shape looked very familiar. Approaching it, she realized she was looking at another coffin built in the center of the room. *Wonder who this is.* She wanted to know, but she didn't want to find out. She'd seen enough corpses, both physical and spectral, these last weeks to fill her sleep with nightmares for years to come.

It was funny that days ago, Luke had complained of her drinking. The behavior was something she hadn't even noticed she'd increased, but, in fact, it all lined up. Ever since that one night, that first encounter with Eileen's ghost, Katherine had definitely felt the increasing need to self-medicate.

She approached the coffin. *Maybe if I avert my eyes.* She tried to tell herself that she didn't *need* to see the body, assuming the coffin contained one. She could simply retreat upstairs, tell the guys what she'd found, call the police, and have that be it.

*Come on, Kat. You know you're not gonna do that.* She sighed in frustrated defeat, knowing her impulse was right. If for no other reason, she was already unraveling this particular mystery of the mansion, so she might as well see it to fruition.

Her feet bumped up against the side of the concrete coffin. *'Kay, how we gonna do this?* She shone her light into the coffin, but did not follow with her gaze. At the edge of her peripheral vision, she noticed a metallic sparkle. *Is that the coffin's back? This one also made of polished silver?*

It was one of the stranger things that she and Kirk's guys had found in Eileen's tomb. That the back of her coffin had a plate of pristine silver, looking exactly like a mirror. Then just the other day, Katherine had discovered two silver bands that led away from Eileen's former coffin, into the tomb's wall, off to some other place below the mansion she hadn't yet seen.

She ignored the silver glint for the moment. She eased her eyes over the coffin's edge. She stopped. *All right, you're gonna see bone, so just, ya know, deal with it.*

White. It was so much lighter than the color of the coffin's side and the surrounding wall that it almost seemed to glow. Creases, folds, and waves. Organic. *It's cloth!* For the moment, she was immeasurably relieved that at least for now, she wouldn't have to see another pile of bones and desiccated flesh. Cloth, even hundred-year-old cloth, she could handle.

She let her eyes take in a little more. *That's a sleeve. Right. So it is another body. But wait. Why is this one clothed?* She could no longer help it. She had to know. She raised her flashlight to focus on the entire corpse and ventured a look.

It was a woman. She was remarkably well preserved. In fact, Katherine recognized only a few signs of death and decay. The woman didn't look as frightening as most Halloween masks. Her face was pale. The skin had tightened around her skull. Her lips had receded from her teeth and gums. Her cheeks had hollowed. The dried remains of her eyes had sunken deep into their sockets. Her hair had been done up in a tight bun around the scalp which, with postmortem skin dehydration, now hung loosely from her skull.

*Oh my God, it's her!* Katherine recognized that face not only from the family portrait she'd seen in the gallery upstairs and the pictures in the Blackstone wing of the Portland Art Museum, but also in the vision Eileen had given her. *I'd recognize that stern, non-smiling mouth anywhere, Gloria. What the hell are you doing down here? And how did you get here? I don't see any stab wounds. No signs of blunt force trauma.* "Natural causes?" The notion sounded silly the instant it left her lips.

Movement. Directly in front of her.

She raised her flashlight to focus on the wall ahead. She then felt that now too familiar open-refrigerator chill run down her spine. Before her, there was a shadow on the wall. It was as clear as if someone were standing right in front of her flashlight. Much like with her first encounter with Eileen, this shadow looked like the fuzzy silhouette of a person. A woman.

Because Katherine had already witnessed Eileen move on, and because she was only aware of one other woman who likely hadn't, she spoke the name she was sure belonged to this shadow. "Gloria?"

The shadow was silent. It didn't move a centimeter.

"It's you, isn't it?" Katherine pointed at the corpse. "This is you."

The shadow said nothing. It still made no movement.

"Why are you down here? Why aren't you in the family cemetery?" In fact, since Gloria's body was here, then who the hell *was* buried in her grave?

The shadow remained infuriatingly silent.

"Why are you still here? Why haven't you moved on? No one murdered you."

That chill grew much more intense. It no longer felt like someone had opened a refrigerator, but that she had stepped inside one, closed the door, and torn off all her clothes. "Ow! Damn it!" She could only take this for a few more seconds before she'd have to run back upstairs. Though she didn't intend it, her tone harshened. "Huh? Why are you still here?"

Ten white points appeared where the shadow's hands were. Thinking back on her first encounter with Eileen, Katherine guessed Gloria was attempting her own contact, outstretched hands first.

"Yeah, come on, Gloria. Come on out!" Katherine wasn't sure why she was feeling so bold. Maybe because she already knew so much more about Gloria than she had about Eileen when she'd first made contact. The fact remained, Katherine was still alone at the bottom of Gloria's tomb. On Gloria's turf. If Gloria could harm her, there most likely wasn't much Katherine could do about it.

Those white points—fingertips—pushed and prodded into the bright circle of Katherine's flashlight. Gloria was struggling.

"Kat?" Shane called from upstairs.

Katherine looked up toward his voice. "One second!"

The chill vanished. She was no longer standing inside a proverbial refrigerator. She looked forward again.

The shadow was gone.

"Crap! No!" Katherine shouted at the blank wall.

"You okay?" Shane asked.

"Yeah, I'm...! Just one sec." *You should get back up. You found out what you wanted to know. They're probably worried sick.* Disappointed, her flashlight sank till its light circle grazed the edge of the coffin's wall. She started back toward the staircase.

She stopped. *The silver.* She shone her light toward the foot of the coffin. She found two bands embedded in the floor that led from the coffin to the wall. *Into the mansion.* What was this apparatus? What was its purpose? She'd have to find out some other day.

She located the bottom steps and began her ascent. She again tried to keep count of them, but again failed. Luckily, though, the climb back up seemed like it took a lot less time than the way down. Before she knew it, a dim rectangle opened up onto the familiar walls of the entryway hall and the many eager, relieved faces of Kirk's crew.

"What...?" Shane stepped forward. "What did you find?"

*What do I tell him? Another body?* She called up to Kirk. "You can release it now."

"You got it."

The open portion of the staircase's wall slid back into place, concealing the tomb's entrance.

"I'd better call Jordan," Katherine said. "And the police."

## 15

"Wait, what?" Jordan asked over Katherine's earbuds. He didn't sound as manic as he had, but now was almost worse. He sounded distracted. Very distracted. And for that with which she needed his help, she did not need him distracted.

"There's another body." She was on her phone several yards down the road from the mansion's gate. It was barely midday and already so much had happened.

"No, I understood you, Kat, I just—Another—! What the—?"

"Right after I get off the phone with you, I'm calling the police."

His focus snapped to attention. "Calling the police? Why?"

"Because it's a crime scene, Jordan. Again."

"God, how many more bodies are you gonna find up there?"

*Probably a few.* She didn't know, but if the pattern she'd so far seen was any indication—one body per tomb beneath two out of four of the mansion's towers, all of which together matched the pendant's symbol—then there were two more bodies waiting for her. "I don't know." She was telling the truth, if holding back her theory as to what else they'd find.

"If a bunch of cops go crawling around up there, how am I gonna have the place ready for Halloween?"

*You can't be serious.* "Well, having the mansion ready for a Halloween event was always going to be a significant challenge."

"I already hired an agency!"

"For what?"

"Publicity, Kat! And setup! And whatever the hell else these agencies do!"

*I warned you!* "Can you get a refund?"

"Yeah, I just go up to the returns desk of their customer service department, show them my receipt and the card I used, and that should do the trick!"

"How much are you out?"

"Doesn't matter. Maybe I can still salvage it. I dunno. What's this gonna do to your sales of the furniture and stuff?"

She thought about that for a second. "Actually, it kinda helps."

"Oh?" His tone brightened right up.

"I mean, as silly as it sounds, any collector who hears about the mansion and its storied history will probably be more attracted to the whole thing."

"Are you saying that finding two bodies up there will raise the price?"

"In a manner of speaking, yes."

"How many more bodies are up there?"

"I don't know. I need to call the cops."

"Wait. If a story of multiple murders can help sell stupid couches, then it'd definitely help sell the place as a Halloween destination!"

"Jordan, I don't think you wanna go down that road."

"I gotta call the agency! Let me know if anything else comes up or if you need help with the cops."

"Jordan, listen to me. I really don't think you should—"

The line clicked. He was gone.

She finished her sentence anyway. "Try to sell the mansion based on dead bodies." She could feel a headache rising. Police involvement was going to slow down her original job of moving out and selling his antiques. His little idea of turning the mansion into a Halloween party was only going to complicate that. And even if both didn't, his constantly shifting whims certainly would.

*A party. Both Vernon's and Gloria's ghosts present. This is not gonna be good. You know what? Just call the police and get it over with.* It was something she had to do anyway, so she took comfort in the procedure of it.

She dialed 9-1-1. "Hi. I'm calling to report a very old murder."

---

"What?" Mac asked.

"What's going on?" Ross asked.

"So we're done?" Dennis asked.

"We still getting paid?" Shane asked.

"You found a what?" Randy asked.

"Guys! Let her speak," Kirk ordered.

They were all assembled at the bottom of the entryway's staircase. Katherine had just informed them they were done for the day, even though they hadn't finished the work they expected.

"We've hit a snag," Katherine said.

The guys nodded their collective understanding.

"Cops are on their way to take care of things." Before the guys threw another round of questions at her, she continued. "Shane, Dennis, Randy, and, of course, Kirk, it's like when we brought in the jackhammer." She was referring to the day they'd discovered Eileen's remains.

"Jackhammer?" Mac asked.

"What's going on?" Ross repeated.

"So we're gonna need to clear everything out, clean up, all that, before the cops arrive," Katherine said. "Though they are gonna wanna take statements. Don't worry about that. You guys didn't do anything wrong. Won't be much of a statement to make. Once we're done with all that, we drop the stuff off, go home."

Shane looked like he was desperate to ask about pay again.

"You will be compensated for the whole day." As soon as she said it, Katherine realized that was going to be another headache-inducing conversation with Jordan, but the fact was, such a promise now would provide the proverbial lubricant she needed for the guys to finish up their work.

The guys all high-fived each other.

"So let's just get done as much as we can before the cops show. All right?" she asked.

The guys murmured their understanding and got back to finishing up their work.

Kirk lingered. "Kat? One second?"

Katherine smiled. "Thought you might ask."

He walked them to the front doors and asked in a hushed tone, "There's gonna be two more, aren't there?"

*Not bad, Kirk.* "If I go looking."

"Who was this body?"

"Gloria."

"She was the matriarch? The one who attempted to strangle Eileen?" He was harkening back to the story Katherine had told him about the vision Eileen had shown her.

"Yeah."

"I don't suppose you know what she was doing in her own tomb, as opposed to—"

"Her own regular, old, run-of-the-mill grave in the family cemetery?"

"Right."

"No, but she, Eileen, the very existence of the tombs, and the mansion looking like this"—she took the pendant out of her purse—"I think are all gonna converge in a big, ol' bulging, festering, stinking mess."

"What was up with this family?"

"I dunno." She put the pendant back in her purse. "You mind if I leave you to it? I wanna take a little walk before the police get here."

"Yeah, no problem. Get some air."

"Thanks, Kirk." She walked outside into the property's ever-lingering twilight. She marched to her right, to the west, straight for the family cemetery.

She didn't run down the hill, but she was in a bit of a hurry. She knew she wouldn't be in trouble if the cops found her hanging out in the cemetery, but she suspected that her presence there would invite a whole slew of more questions she didn't want to answer.

*Why even go? 'Cause I wanna see it. I wanna see her grave.* In a minute, Katherine had reached the cemetery's twisting, looping, wrought-iron fence. She hadn't been here since right after Eileen had shown her the vision of her death.

Katherine climbed over and read the tombstones' names. She descended several rows downhill from where she'd located Silas Blackstone's grave. She scanned more names as she walked from his end almost to the other side. Finally, she found it.

Gloria Blackstone.

Just as with Silas's and the others, the tombstone not only bore Gloria's vital information, but also a bas-relief of her profile. The sculptor had done an amazing job. It looked just like her.

Katherine inspected the ground. There was no sign that the dirt had ever been disturbed. *I'm no mortician, but I'm guessing that grave has only been dug once. That means the coffin's empty. That means that whoever buried the empty coffin was probably Gloria's murderer.* She paused. *Murderer? Why would I assume she was murdered?* She then considered everything she'd experienced so far. In both Eileen's and Gloria's cases, their spirits had hung around the mansion ever since their deaths. In both their cases, their remains were ultimately located inside the mansion. And in

Eileen's case, she had been murdered. So it stood to reason Gloria had been as well.

"But why?" Katherine asked Gloria's stone face. "You weren't stealing a son away. Threatening to blow his fortune on a bakery. You were no threat to anyone, financially or otherwise. Why take you out?"

As she pondered Gloria's fate, she noticed the graves right next to hers. First, there was Reginald Blackstone. Then Vernon Blackstone. And that was it. That was the end of the deceased Blackstones buried in this cemetery.

"Where the hell is Marcus?"

She heard some commotion up the hill and saw that the police had arrived. She started on her way, but threw Gloria's grave a parting comment. "We're not done, Gloria."

---

Katherine's statement to the police was brief. She told them only the facts. She'd had a hunch about the symbol on the plaque on the wall above the entryway staircase. She'd tested her hunch and had found Gloria's body. That was all they needed to know.

She felt the officer had given her a bit of a suspicious attitude, which, in her opinion, was just as ridiculous as when Shane had given her the same attitude when they'd discovered Eileen's body. Both Shane and this officer had looked at Katherine as if she'd gone back in time over a century to murder the two women, then confess now because, of course, that made sense.

While the officer had acted suspiciously, he hadn't gone any further, hadn't requested Katherine not leave town or any of the other cop-based clichés she'd seen in a million hours of true-crime documentaries.

When all was said and done, she waited for Kirk right outside the mansion's front doors. He greeted her with a nod and a smile. Because of his looking more cheerful, she hoped that he was no longer hung up on the question of her and Luke's relationship.

"Ready to get outta here?" Kirk asked.

"Don't have to ask me twice. After you, Mr. Whitehead."

She took his arm. He seemed to welcome it. They headed down the hill.

"So given everything that's going down with this place..." he trailed off, likely hoping she'd pick up the conversational slack.

"Yes?"

"Well, I don't mean to sound selfish or insensitive..."

"But?"

"What's it all mean for the boys and me?"

"You asking whether we're coming out here next weekend?"

"Yeah, I guess I am."

"I'm in touch with buyers."

"And?"

"And I'm gonna be selling soon."

"Great."

"Yeah, provided Jordan doesn't pull the plug on everything."

"Would he?"

"I mean, he's been changing his mind every two seconds, so it wouldn't shock me."

They reached the gate. He opened it for her and closed it behind her. He then opened the passenger side of his truck for her. "I'm thinking drop you off, then drop the stuff off so you don't have to wait for us to drop the stuff off."

She smiled. "Very considerate of you." She was glad that their former rapport seemed to have returned.

"That's me. Considerate Kirk." He jumped in and started up the truck.

After another minute of cruising down Promontory, he looked nervously around, seemingly not wanting to look her directly in the eye. "There's something that's been bugging me."

"Oh?"

"You said that Eileen Byrne contacted you. That was how you knew where she was buried."

"And how she was murdered."

"You also saw the other ghost. Vernon, right?"

"Yeah."

"Did he tell you where to find Gloria?"

"No."

"Did she? Gloria?"

"Uh-uh."

"Yeah, that's where I'm lost. Like, why would Eileen go to all that effort to help you, well, help her, but then Vernon goes to all that effort, except not to have you help him. Then, with Gloria, no effort at all?"

"They never gave me a rulebook."

Kirk's mouth sprang up in an embarrassed grin. "Yeah, I guess they wouldn't."

"Seriously, I'm in almost as much of the dark as you are."

"You think any of them are gonna try to contact you again?"

"I have no doubt."

He finally looked at her and squinted in surprise. "Really?"

"Why wouldn't they? They've all been doing it so far. Why stop?"

"Isn't that... I don't know. How do you deal with that?"

"Clearly I don't, as my nearly totaled car can attest."

"What's the status on that?"

She grinned and teased him. "Already sick of giving me rides?"

He chuckled nervously. "No, no. Just curious."

"Honestly, I've been so distracted, I haven't even checked. I will though. Don't worry."

"No, Kat, it's fine. I like driving you around."

"Good, 'cause I like getting driven." She laughed. "Is it possible for me to say *anything* without it sounding like another hit-on?"

"I don't think so."

They crossed through the heart of Blackstone, and were soon going down the bigger street that turned onto her street. Pulling up to her building, she heaved a sigh. Now that he'd mentioned it, she wondered when the next time would be that one of the Blackstones contacted her.

"You gonna be okay?" he asked.

"You're coming right back." She sounded way too eager. "After you're done. Right?"

He smiled. "Yeah, of course. Just wanna make sure you feel, I dunno, somewhat safe waiting for me."

She nodded, but she did not feel safe. "I'll be fine." She handed him her store keys.

"Be back as soon as I can."

"You better." She smiled and got out of the truck. Waving goodbye, she closed her door.

He waved back and took off.

Entering her unit, she did find she was on edge. She carefully set her purse down on the end of the sofa, and stared out her living room windows at the parking lot below.

She went to her refrigerator and took out a beer. She popped it open and downed a good third. She sat down on her sofa, right next to her purse, and sipped some more.

The apartment was uncomfortably quiet. *Damn it, Kirk. Why'd you have to suggest I'd be contacted again?*

She set her beer on the coffee table, got up, and scoured her apartment for any hiding spirits. She opened closet doors, drawers, even the toilet seat. She felt no chills, heard no noises. She ultimately had a seat back on the sofa.

She picked up her beer and sipped. In the time during her ghost search, the liquid had already warmed to room temperature. She regarded the bottle with a touch of disgust. "Ew." She considered dumping this one and getting a fresh, cold one, but decided against it. "Don't wanna let this one go to waste." She sipped some more.

Her phone *buzzed*, sending her leaping straight out of her skin. "Oh my God!" She set her nearly empty bottle on the coffee table and dug out her phone. She answered with not only more than a hint of irritation, but also without checking who was calling. "Hello?"

"Hey. Everything okay?" Kirk asked.

"Yeah. Sorry. You surprised me, is all."

"We're done here, so I can go ahead and drop off the keys."

"Great!" She sounded so much more relieved than she'd intended. "I'll see you soon."

"Be right there." His smile was audible through his voice. He hung up.

She could not get comfortable, could not feel settled. She could not get the images of the actual remains of Eileen and Gloria, and specters of Eileen's and Vernon's stomach-churning, rotting corpses out of her head.

She went to her living room windows and watched the still parking lot. Staring at it felt better than staring at anything else. She could not wait for Kirk to get here. She waited for what seemed like three hours. Finally, she stood in front of her buzzer and stared at it, waiting for it to alarm her to his arrival.

Though already waiting for it, it still surprised her when the buzzer blared.

She answered. "Hey."

"Hey. I'm here." He looked and sounded as if he were waiting for her to come down and meet him.

She was feeling both desperate and bold. "I want you to come up," she stated as a matter of fact.

"Yeah." His tone sounded almost nervous. "Buzz me up."

*Oh right. That would be helpful.* She pressed the button. The buzzer disconnected.

She walked to the front door, or rather strutted. She was thirsty, and she intended to have herself a drink.

He knocked on the door. She opened it, but didn't invite him in.

"Keys." He held them out.

She didn't accept them. She merely issued orders. "Come in. Close the door."

He did as he was told, still holding the keys out. She left him at the door, crossing to the living room windows. She didn't face him, preferring to keep her eyes on the ground below, partly to present him with a mysterious air.

He did not disappoint. He walked up right behind her. "Did you, uh, want your keys?" He jingled them for emphasis.

She didn't face him. She ordered again. "Coffee table."

He walked very slowly over to the table and placed the keys. He just as slowly walked back and stood behind her. "So..."

She turned around and looked up at him. Directly into his eyes. She swam in them for seemingly endless moments.

Nothing more needed to be said as they fell into each other.

---

Katherine and Kirk lay sprawled and sweaty among her tossed and twisted sheets. She laid her head on his chest. He stroked her hair. It had been epic. Absolutely epic. And exactly what she'd needed for a long, long time.

"That was..." She let out a long, slow exhale.

"Right?"

"I mean..."

"Yeah. Exactly."

"Why did we wait so long?"

"Well, the first-ish opportunity, you were twenty thousand sheets to the wind."

"Oh right."

"Second-ish, your ex interrupted."

"Oh my God. Right! Luke! Arg!"

"Then I dunno about you, but for me, it's been a little awkward ever since."

She burrowed her cheek into his chest. "Yeah, for me too."

"Well, hey." He smiled wide. "Finally made it."

"Boy, did we! Where did you learn to—? Like, that one thing? Damn, kid!"

He laughed. "You know, you don't *always* have to remind me of the age difference."

"So it doesn't bother you at all?"

"Did it seem like it did?"

She laughed. "No. Not even a little. In fact, it seemed like it kinda, you know."

"What can I say? Does it bother you?"

"No. No, no, no."

"I just thought maybe with Luke's teasing."

"No. Screw him."

"Eh..."

"You know what I mean."

"Yeah, I know what you mean."

She was already drifting off to the wonderfully gentle sensation of his fingertips on her head. Before she knew it, she was out.

## 16

Katherine and Kirk got up early, so he'd have plenty of time to drive her to her store, then drive himself back to Creek to get ready for work.

With a quick kiss, they said goodbye, and he drove off. She was left alone with her store. The space inside looked eerily desolate. Packed with the Blackstones' furniture and other items, it looked like a condensed miniature version of the mansion, except with a red awning. Just as abandoned. Just as lonely. Just as lost to time.

As she unlocked the door, she decided to give Jordan a call to check in. She knew doing so would almost certainly give her a headache, but she also wanted to know what was going on, what the police had said, whether he was still planning on his silly Halloween event, all of it.

She closed the door behind her. The *click* sounded terrifyingly heavy, as if she'd locked herself into her own tomb. *Keep it together, Kat.* She took out her phone and dialed Jordan. Three rings later, he answered.

"Jesus, I said hold! Oh, he's already held. Hey, Kat?"

"Jordan!" She was trying not to sound too eager, but the fact was, even his voice comforted her in her store's cramped space. "Hey, yeah, it's Kat."

She reached for the lights and flipped the switch, but nothing happened. *What? What's up with the lights? Gonna have to call Dan.*

"Wow, like, the police. I mean, damn. You'd have thought that *I* murdered them," Jordan complained.

"Sorry to hear that. What's going on?"

"Nothing, just the whole damn property is being considered a crime scene and Halloween's only three days away."

*Does that mean you're dropping your stupid party idea?*
"Yeah, that sounds frustrating."

"'Frustrating.' You better believe it. I told the cops all about my upcoming plans. They so did not care. 'Sir, this is the second body found on your property.' Yeah, dude, I know! How you think *I* feel about that?"

*Huh, sounding like the party's out!* She wasn't sure if she should ask. "I mean, you know, they are right."

"The good news is you were totally right."

*Oh no. About what?* "Yeah?"

"Yeah, the agency? They're all over the two murders. They're like, 'Instagram's gonna flip!'"

"Actually, Jordan, I suggested that about the antiques, not the mansion for Halloween—"

"Exactly, Kat! The mansion for Halloween! It's gonna be a friggin' blowout! Blow-out!"

She sighed hard and hoped he hadn't heard. "So am I still...?"

"Oh yeah. You do you. Pack stuff, sell stuff, whatever. Just, uh, hey, I'm gonna need you to do me a little favor."

*Oh God, no.* "Yeah? What's that?"

"I'm gonna need you there."

She didn't want to pursue this line of questioning, but felt she had no choice. "Where?"

"The mansion! Halloween!"

"I thought you said the cops—"

"Oh, don't worry about that. My lawyers will take care of them."

"So you're gonna have a Halloween party at an active crime scene?"

"Insane, right? Friggin' brilliant!"

"Um, why would you want me there?"

"You found the bodies!"

"Right, but—"

"You add flavor, authenticity."

"So I'm gonna stand around and, what, hold up a sign saying It Was Me?"

He laughed. "Kat, you're hilarious. Love that about you. No, you're gonna be on hand for guests, influencers, VIPs, you know, to tell your story."

"My story?"

"Yeah! About how you found the bodies. Oh, but make it really interesting. Take epic ass-tons of artistic license."

*Actually, Jordan, I don't think that'll be necessary.* "So I'm gonna stand around like a costumed character at a theme park waiting for photo ops?"

He laughed even louder. "No! No, no, no, no, no." He paused. "Oh wait. Yes! Yes, that's exactly what I need you to do. Yes, costumed character. In fact, can you get a costume?"

She couldn't believe her ears. Did he honestly expect her to hang out and perform a one-woman show of her experiences digging up Eileen and discovering Gloria? *Who am I kidding? Of course he expects me to do that!* "You mean like a witch or black cat or Grim Reaper?"

"No! No, no, no! Don't be ridiculous."

"That's a relief."

"No, like, a nineteen twenties wealthy matron!"

"Like Gloria."

"Who?"

"Your great-great-whatever grandmother? Whose body we found yesterday? I showed you her jewelry box a few weeks ago?"

# THE POSSESSION OF BLACKSTONE MANSION

"Oh right! Yes! Exactly like her! In fact, the more like her you can look, the better."

"So you want me to look like the body we found telling the story of how we found... the body?"

He sounded like she'd officially gone way over his head. "Whatever you think works. Listen, Kat, I gotta go. Calls to make."

"Jordan, hold on. Do you mind if I bring a plus one?"

"Plus one... Oh, yeah, sure! A date! Yeah, bring whoever."

"It's gonna be Kirk, the guy I hired to move all your stuff."

"Dating the help! Love it! A total blue-collar authenticity angle. Yeah, see if you can get him to dress up as a zombie handyman or something."

"I'll see what I can do."

"Love it, Kat. See you Halloween night!"

"See you then." She hung up. She let her hand that was holding her phone drop to her side as she decided what she wanted to do next.

She looked out over the mass of pieces, taking up most of the walkable space in her store. While she'd already done a preliminary mental catalog as Kirk and his crew had moved the items, she decided to do a more formal one now on her phone.

As she got started, she kept thinking about the various things that had happened the last few days, and her mind landed on the mansion's floor plan and the pendant's symbol. She remembered that number she'd found of the county's records department.

She swiped her list of the mansion's pieces aside and called the number.

A bored-sounding female voice answered. "Records."

"Hi, I don't know if I'm calling the right number. I'm looking for information on a property in eastern Clackamas county, near Mt. Hood. Probably ZIP 97023."

"Address?"

"Um, wow, that's a good question. The street is Promontory Drive."

"Number?"

"Try one."

Fingers tapped keys on the other end. "No listing."

"It's an old property. Technically still abandoned. Would the name help? Current owner?"

"Maybe."

"Jordan Blackstone."

More typing. "No listing."

"Really? I've been there a bunch of times."

"I'm not saying it doesn't exist, ma'am, just that there's no listing."

"Why would that be?"

"Any number of reasons. How old's the house?"

"At least before 1900."

"Before 1850?"

"Maybe. Probably."

"Yeah, county records don't go before 1859, the year of the state's founding."

"Sorry. I don't understand. Why does that matter?"

"Well, any record that might've been kept may have been with the territory before statehood. Then, it could've been lost in that transfer between the two governments. Or any time since. Moves. Fires. Any number of reasons why the record could've been lost, assuming we ever had one."

"I see. So no way of checking out a floor plan."

"You could always ask the owner."

"I don't think he has one."

"He could have the property surveyed."

"I doubt he'd be willing to pay for that."

"Unfortunately, then, unless you have more specific information I can look up, and that's assuming the record even exists."

"No, that's fine. Thanks for your help."

"Have a good day." She hung up.

*Great. So no way to know what those silver connectors between the tombs are for. Unless I ask Jordan to have someone look at them.* "I'd have to tell him why."

She continued her catalog. Sofas, harpsichord, tables, ashtray stands. She sent Aleeyah a text alerting her what she had and asking when she wanted to drop by.

> Darling! How's tomorrow or Wed?

> Either's fine by me. I'll be here.

> Let me book my flight, make those other pesky arrangements, and get back to you.

> Sounds good, Leeyah. Talk soon.

> Over and out!

Katherine sent more texts updating other contacts, then decided to have an early, very long lunch.

Within minutes, she'd walked to the diner, parked herself in a corner, and ordered her lunch of a Greek omelet and hot cocoa. Because she had so little to do before Aleeyah and others arrived to duel to the death over the mansion's pieces, she decided to take a healthy amount of time with each step. She'd chill at the diner for a total of two hours. She'd take leisurely walks around the square. She'd return to her store where she'd take a few pictures of each item to send to her contacts, get them all worked up before their arrival. Finally, around 5:00, she'd text Kirk to come pick her up and ask him to take her back to his place. That was assuming he'd be down for that.

# THE POSSESSION OF BLACKSTONE MANSION

Hours later, she returned from her latest stroll around the town square to her store, awash in the orange light of the fading sunset. Stepping inside, it hit her how alone she was in the dark with all these mansion relics.

She took out her flashlight and turned it on. *Guess I'll double check to see if I missed any piece.* She walked forward, but only managed two steps before she'd bumped into something. Her light revealed it to be a leather chair, very much like the first one she'd encountered at the mansion. *One of those Loscudo chairs. With others, it'll command at least ten thousand. Maybe as high as fifty.*

Movement. Ahead of her. Somewhere in the back.

*Did I see something or only think I saw something?* She decided to keep focusing on the pieces in front of her. She moved past the chair. Directly behind it stood a black marble ashtray stand. "Hope Leeyah can find an eager buyer for that." She wasn't actually going through an internal process of where best to sell the ashtray. She was talking out loud not only to distract herself, but to keep herself company.

Movement. Much closer. To her right.

She lifted her flashlight, but saw nothing other than a wall of furniture and smoking paraphernalia. There were no shadows or shadows in shadows, as she'd already seen in the mansion.

"What else do we have here?" She hadn't even yet focused on another piece.

A sudden, intense chill rose directly behind her. She felt the back of her head and neck go numb.

*He's here.* She heard that same creaking groan, but she tried to pay attention to any other sound rather than allow her mind to confirm. Was that a distant car horn honking? Nope. *Great. Just me and him. And the only way outta here is to turn around.*

She twisted her body toward the front door. She wasn't scared in the same way as she had been during her first encounter with Eileen's ghost. This was more she simply didn't want to deal with what she knew she was about to confront. The cold, the rot, the rage or whatever it was these spirits felt. She wanted to push past it and leave.

Her light caught something dark, twisted, dangling. It was sinew or rot-encrusted bone or something else awful. She now wanted to back away, but was afraid that if she did, she'd trip over one of the pieces and knock it down, or worse, break it.

The repeated mirrored curves of... a rib cage. *All right, Vernon.* That groan was even louder, now that the entity was standing directly in front of her, now that she had no possible nearby distractions to take her mind away.

The location of the sound lowered and, as incredible as it seemed, drew closer. Up to her right ear.

She heard the popping and cracking of bone as she imagined a jaw moving up and down in an attempt at articulation. She heard deep, guttural moans. And that stench. That awful smell that had so tortured her nose in the first encounter with Eileen's ghost.

Suddenly, Katherine had enough. Forgetting all about the possibility of tripping backwards over one of the pieces, she stepped back and pointed her flashlight up at where she thought the skull might be.

She was not wrong. Her whole field of vision filled with the black pits of empty eye sockets, the half rotted nasal ridge, and the bulging, black chunks of teeth that lined the nasty grin of a jawbone.

"What?" she demanded of the specter. "What do you want? What do you want me to do? What do you...?"

*Buzz!* Her phone throbbed. She was so shocked, and relieved, that she nearly fell over. Her shaking fingers clumsily slid it out of her pocket. Kirk. Her eyes lifted above the phone to the space beyond.

The ghost was gone.

Her hands and voice still shaking, she answered. "Hey."

"Hey, you okay? You sound—"

"Kirk? I need a favor. It's gonna sound nuts, but I need it."

"Um, okay, sure, uh, what do you need me to do?"

## AUGUSTINE PIERCE

"How far away are you?"

## 17

Katherine and Kirk were in his truck on Promontory, with the mansion only a few minutes away.

"Maybe I'm just dumb," he said.

"You're not dumb."

"Well, maybe I am because I don't get why we're going back, especially now that it's a crime scene."

"Vernon's contacted me three times. I don't know what he wants. I don't know what he needs. But since the two bodies we've uncovered have been Eileen and Gloria, not men, I assume he wants me to find his."

"Didn't Eileen give you a vision that told you, like, her whole story, how she was murdered, everything?"

"Yeah. Why?"

"Well, that means these spirits can do that, so why hasn't he?"

"I don't know. Maybe..."

"Three times."

"Including tonight, yeah."

"She only appeared once before she showed you what you needed to know."

"And Gloria never contacted me, not fully, before we found her."

"Yeah, it's just after Eileen's case, it doesn't make a lot of sense."

"The only obvious direction I have is the remaining towers, their symbols."

"If you think it's what you have to do."

"It's the only thing I can think of."

They soon arrived at the gate. Crime scene tape had been placed over its doors. They got out. She approached the tape.

"I assume you're not gonna let a little crime scene contamination stop you," he said.

She had the impulse to tug at the tape, but resisted it. *Ironic that I don't wanna touch the tape, but have zero problem mucking up everything behind it.* "Believe it or not, I don't love the idea. Hoping that Jordan's lawyers can get us out of anything we need to be gotten out of."

"That's assuming he won't sic them on us."

Kirk wasn't wrong. Only weeks ago, Jordan had been threatening Katherine with legal action. They seemed to be in a pretty good place now, but she could see him doing the same thing again.

She reached past the tape to push the right gate door open. Its echoing creak yowled.

"I swear I only notice that when no one else is around," Kirk said.

"Same here." She half crouched, half ducked under the tape and slid in.

"Need any help?"

"Uh-uh." She smiled back. "Do you?"

"Think I can manage." He shuffled under.

They hiked up the hill in silence. She kept thinking about his questions. *Why has Vernon contacted me three times? Why didn't Gloria give me a vision?* Katherine didn't know. What she did know was that any remaining tombs were the next logical step.

They reached the front doors and found another layer of crime scene tape. This band hung lower, so they only had to step over.

Inside, she took out and turned on her flashlight. She located the door to the right of the staircase, which she knew would lead to the east tower. He scanned the entryway hall more casually.

"Seems a lot bigger when it's just the two of us," he said.

"Come on." She led them through the door.

They walked to the west-east hallway and turned right. They soon reached the east tower's doors. She opened them and marched straight to the symbol on the other side of the room. She nodded as she shone her light on it.

"What you expected?" he asked.

"Yeah, I saw it the other day."

"So, what do we do now?"

"We push the symbol in, then to the right, where the missing part is."

"Missing part?"

"All the mansion's symbols are based on the pendant I found. If we lined the pendant up with this one, it'd be missing the right part."

"And where's the door open from?"

She pointed to a section of the wall to the left of the spiral staircase's first steps. "Right about there."

"So we just push the button and the door opens up?"

"That's what's happened so far." She pressed her hands against the symbol. It gave easily. She could feel it slide into the wall.

He joined her and pressed his hands where he could fit them.

"All right, hold that," she said.

"Yes, ma'am."

She went to the part of the wall where she expected it to open. She took a quick breath. While she'd done this twice now, she still didn't love the descent into the stale dark that followed. "Ready."

She heard his hands push the symbol to the right. The switch's mechanism popped and clacked in the wall. Stone ground.

She lifted her flashlight to where she expected the wall to open. A rectangular portion receded only about half a foot from where she had her light pointed.

She turned around to instruct him. "Keep it pressed. I'll be back."

"Kat, are you absolutely sure? We could wait till daytime. I could call the guys."

"Whatever this is, I want it done. Besides, what do I need your guys for when I have you?" She grinned.

He nodded and shrugged. "I'll hold down the fort."

She saluted and walked into the passage.

Exactly as she'd assumed, it was a staircase curving down into the stony dark. It so far looked like, if opposite to, the design she'd found in Eileen's tomb. After only a few seconds, she'd reached the bottom.

She approached the concrete coffin. *All right, either Reginald or Vernon. Or who knows? Anybody else.*

She took a steadying breath. Even after having seen Eileen's and Gloria's remains, and Vernon's skeletal specter, she could not get used to finding corpses in these dark chambers.

She lifted her flashlight. The beam crawled up and over the coffin's edge. It slid onto dark folds. Cloth. The tail coat of a gentleman's evening wear.

While the edges had fringed from over a century of having laid in this tomb, they hadn't decomposed into scraps.

She drew her light across the corpse's torso, its chest. There she saw it.

A hole.

It was on the left side of the chest, near the collar bone. It was perfectly round, as if it had been precisely measured. On closer inspection, it wasn't just a hole through the cloth, but deep into the body. Its edge was singed and beveled. An exit wound.

*He was shot!* While she was no doctor, she was sure a bullet had punctured this man's left lung near the top of the organ. In fact, she was certain the cause of death was he'd drowned in his own blood as it filled his lung. *Terrible way to go. Killer wanted him to suffer.*

She prepared herself to see his face. While Gloria's hadn't been awful—a relatively preserved visage when compared to Eileen's remains—it was still deeply disturbing to behold in these dark, silent tombs.

*All right, here goes.* She aimed her light at the man's face. *Oh my God! It's Reginald!* Just as with his mother's head, the skin of his face had tightened over his skull. The remains of his eyes had shrunken into their sockets. His nostrils had widened to reveal a triangular nasal cavity. The skin around his mouth had receded to expose his teeth and gums. His face, though, was still recognizable from the family pictures, the photographs from the Portland Art Museum, and from the vision Eileen had given Katherine.

This was Reginald. Someone had shot him in the back. If Katherine didn't know better, she could have sworn that an expression of shock and anger still lingered on his face. *He knew his killer. Trusted him.*

She stood back from the body, from the coffin. She'd been so taken with what the corpse had revealed that she'd hardly noticed the silver plate upon which the body lay. She also hadn't thought about whether Reginald's spirit was hanging around, watching her.

She lifted her flashlight to the wall and scanned all around. There was no movement. There were no shadows. *Looks like it's just me. For now.*

She retreated from the coffin and in her light's slide across the floor, she only barely noticed the same silver bands extending from the coffin's foot, across the floor, into the wall. *Gotta figure that out. Must mean something.*

She climbed the stairs back to the surface. She announced her presence, so she didn't freak Kirk out. "I'm back."

"What'd you find?" He released the symbol-switch.

She heard the open section of the wall grind back into place, hidden from plain view. There was something extremely disconcerting about that sound. Its heavy closure, its finality. That beyond it, a body had laid undisturbed for over a century.

She walked forward a few steps to get away from the closed wall. "What I expected. A body. Reginald. That's so far Eileen, Reginald's fiancée, Gloria, and now Reginald himself."

"How many more of these?"

"Just the north tower."

"Who do you think'll be there?"

"Only one left. Gloria's husband Vernon, who almost left her for Eileen, before, well, the whole family murdered the poor girl."

"And no idea why all these family members are buried inside the mansion rather than in the actual cemetery?"

"Nope. None. I mean, there must've been a reason someone went to all the trouble to build these tombs, bury the bodies, and seal them back up so no one would ever find them."

"No one except you."

"And that was only through Eileen's help."

Katherine headed out of the east tower and into the hallway that led to the north tower, the location of the final tomb.

They walked in silence until they reached the north tower. She opened the double doors.

"It's not like the others," he observed.

"No. I was guessing it was some kind of study."

He looked around, but didn't see this tower's symbol. "Where is it?"

"In there." She pointed to the left corner at which the flat and semicircular walls met. "Sliding bookshelf."

"How many more secrets does this place have?"

"Right?"

He gripped the bookshelf and eased it aside. He gasped at the reveal of the shadowy chamber within. "What is this?"

"Private study? Vernon's? Maybe every Blackstone patriarch's back to Silas?"

Kirk faced her. "So you've been in here?"

"Where I found the pendant."

He nodded and gave her an admonishing grin as if to say "So you have been sneaking around."

He entered the study. She followed him to give him as much light as possible.

"There it is." He pointed to this tower's symbol. "Same as last time? Press and push?"

"I think so."

"Where's the opening gonna be?"

"That is a good question." She stepped out of the study and looked around the rest of the room.

Unlike the entryway hall, and west and east towers, this room had no bifurcated or spiral staircase at whose base she could deduce the presence of some hidden passage.

"Maybe you should stand back." He pointed to her feet, planted at about the middle of the room.

"Yeah." She looked down at her own feet. "Good idea." She walked back to the room's double doorway.

"Ready?"

She nodded. "Hit it."

He pressed the symbol into the wall, then pushed it up.

They heard stone grind and wood scrape. It sounded like it was coming from all around the room. She half expected to see the entire wall recede, to reveal a vast network of hidden passages.

They heard a loud *thunk*.

She saw nothing obvious happen. "Where is it?"

"I dunno."

A series of *thunks* followed.

"Something's happening, but..." she said.

A sofa situated in the middle of the room facing the left side began to tip forward.

"What the...?" she asked.

"What's goin' on?"

"Nothing! Stay there!" She ran to the sofa and lifted its front to keep it flush with the floor. Looking down, she saw the source of the sounds.

# THE POSSESSION OF BLACKSTONE MANSION

A section of the floor, as wide as the steps in the tombs, was descending to form a spiral staircase. She looked to her right. As each step continued downward, the one in front of it began to lower. *It's, like, automated!* For modern technology, such a sight would have been impressive, but for such a mechanism to be over a century old and still function with, she guessed, minimal maintenance, it was amazing.

She relaxed her grip on the sofa, and as she faced the bottom of the staircase, she heard wood and cloth scrape against stone as the piece of furniture fell behind her.

"Kat?" Kirk asked.

"All good!"

The *thunks* ceased. The revealed staircase, concentric with the left half of the semicircular wall, descended a full seven feet underground.

"Wow." She walked down the shadow-draped steps.

"Wait!" Kirk insisted, his hands still pressed onto the symbol.

"What?"

"You sure it's safe?"

"Looks like the others."

"Doesn't mean it's safe, Kat."

"It's just gonna be another body."

"That's not what concerns me."

"Just hold on to the trigger or whatever. I'll be fine."

He raised his eyebrows in deep skepticism, but did as she requested. "You sure you're sure?" he asked.

"Yeah." She knew he was looking out for her, but she couldn't help feeling eager to uncover this final tomb.

Reaching the bottom of the visible part of the staircase, she passed into the tunnel that continued below.

"What do you see?" he called.

"It's fine, Kirk. Just more stairs."

She followed the steps deeper and deeper underground. She didn't know whether it was just her anticipation of this tomb or whether it really was the deepest one so far. While she expected to find another space of similar design and dimensions to the previous three, she hoped for a greater—she didn't even know what to call it—revelation?

She reached the ground. To her disappointment, this tomb looked exactly like the others. A vaulted room with a concrete coffin sitting at its center.

She went straight up to the coffin. She no longer felt any fear or disgust at what she might find inside. She raised her flashlight to inspect its contents.

A pair of black leather cap toe boots. A pair of dark gray trousers. A waistcoat. An evening jacket. Then she saw the mummified face she'd seen at King's

Lanes, the back of her car, and in her store. It was Vernon Blackstone.

Unlike with Reginald's corpse, though, Vernon didn't look shocked or angry. As far as Katherine could tell, he looked deeply sad. While she lacked many of the details of the family's story, she imagined he'd tried to hold his family together, through his affair with Eileen, the challenges that had arisen because of it, and finally, her ensuing death.

While Katherine knew Vernon had ultimately been complicit in Eileen's murder, she couldn't help but feel just a little sorry for him. "The last patriarch of the great Blackstone dynasty," she informed the corpse.

She lifted her flashlight to the opposite wall. "You here, Vern?" She heard no groans. She saw no shadows in shadows. As far as she could tell, he was not. *Why's he hiding now?*

Kirk shouted. She couldn't tell what he'd said.

"Kirk?" She approached the bottom of the staircase.

He didn't answer. Then she heard the noise that only moments ago had so excited her with what it would reveal.

*Thunk! Thunk! Thunk!* They were coming from above. In quick succession.

Immediately following those sounds came ones that set off her survival instincts. It was stone grinding against stone.

*Wait, that's...!*

She ran up the stairs, but soon found what she hadn't yet been willing to admit to herself, what Kirk had tried to warn her about.

The step that above ground had been the final one to lower, and thus reveal the descending staircase's passage underground, had risen again. It now stood before her, a solid stone wall with no seam, switch, or other device by which it could be lowered.

She was trapped.

## 18

"Kirk! Kirk!" Katherine shouted into the stone wall in front of her. She knew it was a futile gesture. She knew there was no way he could hear her, and worse, even if he could, she was sure there was nothing he could do.

She pressed her hands against the stone. She knew this, too, would do nothing, but she had the instinct to feel something solid, perhaps solely as a reminder that this world was real, that she wasn't dreaming or hallucinating.

Her mind spun. *I'm here. He's up there. What happened? Did he let go? No! He never would've let go of the symbol. Hell, he was the one who warned me against coming down here. So what happened?* She didn't know, and that's what was driving her nuts, beyond her current situation.

With a quick breath, she decided that standing next to this impenetrable wall was accomplishing nothing. She turned around and with her flashlight went back down the stairs to the foot of Vernon's coffin.

Pointing her light lazily past it, her eyes scanned the darkness beyond the beam. She wasn't looking for anything in particular. She was trying to maintain calm and focus. *Probably got a few hours of air since Vernon's not breathing.*

She took out her phone and checked its battery. It was down to thirty percent. She supposed that if her flashlight's batteries failed, she'd still have her phone. For a little while anyway.

She walked around the coffin's left side, up to where she stood next to Vernon's mummified skull. *Why have you all reached out? What is it you've wanted? Who did this to each of you? Why?*

As she studied Vernon's dead face and thought about how sad he looked, she again noticed the sheen of the silver plate beneath his body. *And what the hell is up with the coffins?*

She stepped away and inspected the floor past its foot. As with all the others, Vernon's had two silver bands leading into the wall. She followed them and knelt next to the spot where they entered the stone. She shone her light along the length of the bands. *Why do they all go to the center of the house?*

She sat next to the wall and dug into her purse. She took out the pendant and held it over her light. "Each tomb has a body." She touched a fingertip to each of the pendant's circles at each point of the triangle and V. "Each body lies on a silver plate. Each plate connects to..." She traced an invisible line from each of the points' circles to the center of the pendant. "Gotta be something there." *But what? And how do I get there?*

She picked herself up. The tomb's inevitably depleting oxygen was weighing heavily on her. *Before I do anything else, I gotta get outta here.* She walked along the tomb's perimeter and scanned every inch of its surface, or at least every inch she could see under the beam of her flashlight.

It was completely useless. There wasn't any sign of any other way to get out of here but for the stairs she'd come down.

She parked at the coffin's foot. *Can't call Kirk. Can't text him. And*—she checked her phone's battery, now twenty-eight percent—*this thing'll die before I know it.*

Panic seized her mind. She ran up a few stairs. She stumbled and tripped. She climbed the rest until she reached the solid stone wall. She hammered her fists and cried Kirk's name over and over.

She heard nothing from the other side. Not Kirk's voice, not the clicking of the staircase's mechanism, nothing at all.

She tried to reason with herself. *He's doing what he can. He's attempting to get it open again. He won't let me die down here.*

## AUGUSTINE PIERCE

The second she thought the "d" word, she lost control. Tears dripped down her cheeks. *What am I doing down here? Why couldn't I have left it well enough alone? Why didn't I listen to Kirk? He was just trying to keep me safe!*

She choked out two sobs, then stopped. *You can't... you can't do anything, Kat. There's no button to press. You've just gotta... you gotta trust that he's doing what he can, that he won't let you die.*

She collapsed next to the wall. She leaned up against it and stretched her legs down the stairs. It wasn't the most comfortable position, but it beat any other she could think of.

With her phone soon to die, she shut it off and put it away. She also turned off her flashlight and sat in the total silent black, wondering when her air would run out.

A second passed. Or a minute. Or an hour. She kept thinking of turning her phone back on to check, but kept deciding not to. *Why bother?* She finally let out a relaxed exhale. *Well, I mean, if this is it, then at least it's not the bottom of a river.*

She made herself as comfortable as she could in the corner between the raised-stair wall and the side of the staircase. She took off her jacket, wadded it up into a makeshift pillow, and stuck it between her head and shoulder.

She relaxed into it. *If I just go to sleep, I won't notice it when it comes.* She shook her head. *No, come on, Kat. Kirk's coming. You'll see.*

Holding on to that pleasant thought, she now felt the fatigue of the day. She closed her eyes. *Just gonna... just gonna...*

Black.

## 19

The sensation of the hard surface sinking behind her and its accompanying *grind* woke Katherine right up. Her eyes snapped open, but that turned out to be a pointless instinct as she still saw nothing but solid black.

"Where...?" She remembered. She was trapped in Vernon's tomb underneath the north tower. The last thing that had crossed her mind before she'd passed out was coming to the very loose grips with the possibility of dying down here, alone—except for Vernon's nearby corpse—in the dark, in the silence, and because of the undramatic cause of lack of oxygen after who knew how many hours?

The lowering wall behind her was telling a different story. As she came to her senses, she realized that the fact of the sinking wall meant she would soon be able to walk up the rest of the spiral staircase out of here, to the ground floor, where she hoped to see Kirk waiting for her.

She was not disappointed.

# THE POSSESSION OF BLACKSTONE MANSION

"Kat?" Kirk asked. "You there? Can you hear me? Katherine?"

*Why doesn't he just come over?* That was right. He *couldn't!* In order to re-open the mechanically descending staircase into the tomb, he had to press the tower's symbol into the wall and down in order to trigger the entire process.

*So what happened before? Did he just let go?* The exit to the tomb had closed without warning, so she had no idea what had caused it.

She remembered that he'd asked for her. "Yeah! Here! I'm fine! Where are you? I don't see you!"

"I'm, uh, still holding down the fort."

The wall before her had descended back to being a mere step. Behind it, the remaining steps had already settled into their places. All she had to do was leave the tomb.

She eagerly ran up the rest of the steps, where she found the left bookshelf slid away from the study beyond. Kirk stood with both hands pressed against the symbol on the wall. She could hardly see him in the dim light his phone gave off, so she turned her flashlight back on.

She wrapped her arms around him and felt his body relax. She heard the symbol's mechanism *click* inside the wall. She heard the steps behind her rise until they returned to their default positions flush with the rest of the floor, and thus barely detectable.

"Thought I'd lost you," he said.

"Same here."

He turned around and embraced her. They kissed a few quick times. He put his phone back in his pocket.

"What happened?" she asked.

"I don't know. I was pressing the, uh, switch-symbol thing, waiting on you, when the bookshelf slammed shut. It startled me. I let go of the switch, and when I went to look for it again, my phone suddenly got really cold. Like, it burned!"

*Sounds familiar*, she thought, recalling the very first full-on encounter she'd had in the mansion when, though she didn't know it at the time, Eileen had pulled a similar trick on the cake stand that Katherine had found. "Flew outta your hand?"

"I dunno. Didn't exactly see. Whether it flew or I dropped it, it was gone. Had to dig around in the dark to find it. I heard the stairs rise again, and I knew it was closing in on you."

"Yeah, it was scary how quickly it all happened."

"I tried to go back to the wall, to the symbol, press it again, but somehow, I got turned around. Disoriented. I couldn't find it to save my life. That's why it took so long."

"How long was I trapped?"

He dug out his phone and checked the time. "Actually, only about four minutes."

*Four minutes? That's all it took for me to give up, assume I was dead, and pass out?*

"Felt like so much longer."

"Yeah."

"What happened down there?"

"Nothing. Just the steps rose up to walls again, closed up."

"And nothing before then?"

"Found Vernon. That was it." She chose not to go into the silver plate at the bottom of his coffin and the bands that went from there into the wall. It wasn't only that she didn't welcome even more questions that she couldn't answer, but also that she was getting the impression that the more she let Kirk in, the more danger she put him in. That was something she wasn't willing to do.

"So, did you take care of what you wanted to? What we came up here for?"

She wasn't sure how to answer him. Technically, yes. She'd opened the remaining tombs. But having found two more Blackstone family corpses ended up not answering any questions for her. And if she were being honest, she wasn't sure what she had expected to have answered. "I guess. For now."

"Wanna get outta here?"

"Yes."

He took her hand and with both his phone's light and her flashlight, they walked all the way back to the mansion's front doors. The whole way, she kept quiet, thinking about what she'd found tonight and what it meant.

*Gloria, Reginald, and Vernon. All three murdered. At least I think so. Makes sense. All three buried in those strange tombs. Besides Eileen. Marcus was the only other family member living here. Did he do all of it? Wouldn't surprise me. Little creep. But why? When I saw him in Eileen's vision, he didn't seem to be after his family, but if it was him, he murdered each a year apart starting after Eileen.*

Katherine knew the next thing she should do was contact the police and Jordan. Report these latest bodies. After that, though, she wasn't sure where to find her next clues as to what any of this meant. And she hesitated with Jordan. He'd been so, well, pissy when it'd come to the question of anything delaying his little Halloween soirée and she didn't want to risk his firing her over causing yet another delay. At the same time, the law didn't care about his social calendar. There had been multiple murders on this property. Over a century ago, yes, but murders all the same.

*Will that release them? The murdered Blackstones?* It felt trivial, the idea of simply having their bodies moved to their currently empty graves in the family cemetery. It was only down the hill less than half a mile away. It somehow felt so unceremonious.

# THE POSSESSION OF BLACKSTONE MANSION

"How you holding up?" Kirk opened the left front door for her.

"Fine."

"It's just you've been quiet for a while."

"Nothing, just thinking about tonight and what it all means."

"What does it all mean? These bodies? The secret passages? The weird symbol?"

"I have to find more information. There's gotta be something out there. Something I just haven't uncovered yet."

"I'm sure you'll find it. You've found everything else so far."

They headed down the hill to the gate.

"When're you calling the police?" he asked.

"I'll do it tomorrow morning. I don't wanna deal with it right now." She looked up at him, smiled, and squeezed his hand. "I think I need a distraction if you wanted to take us back to your place."

Even under the shadows of the trees, it looked like he was blushing. "Um, sure. Yeah, we can go to my place. I've, uh, got work tomorrow, though."

"I won't keep you up all night. Promise."

## 20

Katherine still lay in Kirk's bed, naked from the previous night's distraction. His apartment was smaller than hers, a little messier, but not nearly as bad as she'd feared the abode of a mid-twentysomething straight guy would be.

He'd already gone to work and had left her with his blessing to help herself to coffee, the meager victuals in his fridge, and to take off whenever she'd wanted, so long as she'd locked the door behind her.

*I'm alone.* She jumped out of bed. Her eyes darted about the room. She saw no sign of Vernon or any other spirit. She ran into the bathroom, but saw nothing suspicious in the mirror either. Then she realized she was staring at her own bare body. Embarrassed, she returned to the bedroom and threw on her clothes.

She looked down at her phone plugged into its charger on the night stand. *God, I don't wanna do this*, she thought, referring to calling Jordan about the latest round of dead-relative discoveries. *Might as well get it over with, Kat.* She picked up the device and tapped his name. It rang three times before he answered.

"Kat! Good morning!" he said. "I was gonna ring you in just a quick sec."

"What? Why?" Then she remembered her manners. "'Morning."

"'Morning! Again! Remember? The electrician's dropping by the mansion. You'll be there, right?"

*Oh my God, I completely forgot! And wait, did I even agree to...?* "Um, be there. That's gonna be a bit of a challenge."

"Why?"

"I'm not exactly close by."

"Where are you?"

"Creek?"

"What are you doing in a creek?"

"No, Creek, Jordan. It's a town a little northwest of Blackstone."

"Oh, well, whatever you're doing in Brook, get your ass out there. We'll be there in about twenty minutes."

"You're gonna be there?"

"Yep!"

"Why?"

"Want somethin' done right..."

She wasn't sure if that was a dig at her. *Not my fault you screwed up the original date!* "It's probably gonna take twenty just to get an Uber."

"Well, then, don't let me slow you down." He hung up without another word.

She listened to the silence of the hung-up line for two seconds before letting out a frustrated sigh.

---

Katherine saw a Portland General Electric van and a neon-blue Ferrari parked several yards downhill from the mansion's gate. She then saw both Jordan and a short, middle-aged man wearing a scraggly beard, a PGE jacket, and a utility belt standing right in front of the gate. Jordan looked very annoyed. The man looked a little overwhelmed. *Probably never seen a house this big, has no clue how he's gonna wire it.* "Here's fine," she told her Uber driver.

The driver parked. "Have a good day."

Katherine got out, finished off the ride on her phone, and waved to Jordan and the electrician.

The Uber drove back down the hill. Katherine silently wished she could've just stayed inside and be driven back to her apartment.

"Took you a while," Jordan complained, not even bothering to hide his annoyance for politeness' sake.

# THE POSSESSION OF BLACKSTONE MANSION

"Twenty from Creek to Blackstone, another ten or so here," Katherine reminded him, also foregoing politeness.

"This is Steven." Jordan only half raised his hand to point to the electrician.

"Call me Steve." He stepped forward and offered Katherine his hand.

*He doesn't seem to care that it's a crime scene. Guess Jordan already covered that?* "'Morning, Steve. I'm Katherine. Kat. Thanks for waiting. Sorry about the delay." She shook his hand.

"Oh, not at all." Steve looked up past the gate at the mansion. "Just admiring your house here."

"My house," Jordan corrected him.

"Right. 'Course," Steve said.

"Well, shall we?" Katherine pointed to the gate.

"After you folks."

Jordan lifted the crime scene tape, opened the gate doors, and marched in.

Katherine found his demeanor a little strange. His frustration at not getting exactly what he wanted literally the second he wanted it wasn't the odd part. His seeming complete disinterest and total lack of curiosity regarding the mansion was throwing her. He'd said that he hadn't been here since he was a kid, and yet he'd hardly looked at the place, even in pride after Steve's reaction. *Man, I wonder if he's ever seen any of his dead relatives or maybe even shadows moving in shadows.*

"This's a mighty big place you got here, Mr. Blackstone," Steve said, sounding bowled over by the mansion's size and design.

"Certainly is," Jordan said, sounding like he was forcing the politeness out of his mouth with a fire engine pump.

"And black!"

"Easier to hide the dirt."

Steve regarded him with genuine intrigue. "That why?"

Jordan looked like he was about to say something über-sarcastic, so Katherine interrupted. "Jordan." She walked right up next to him and spoke quietly, not wanting to tip off Steve, but also wanting to get this over with. "We need to talk about the, uh, basement."

"What about it?" Jordan didn't at all try to keep his voice down.

"I came back here last night." Katherine still maintained her low tone.

Jordan stopped and faced her.

Steve paused his hike, turned around, and waited a few feet away.

"What are you talking about? It's a crime scene," Jordan reminded her.

"I know. I was curious about something," Katherine said.

"What about?"

"There are more... *things* down there."

"What things? More antiques?" Jordan looked hopeful at the thought, then continued on his way.

Katherine and Steve followed.

*Well, technically, the coffins are antiques and their silver plates are undoubtedly worth something. Then again, removing them from the floors of the tombs'll cost more than it's worth.* "Not exactly." She eyed Steve, trying to clue Jordan in on the idea that she wanted to keep this information between them.

They arrived at the front doors.

"So what is it?" Jordan asked, not at all getting the hint.

"Um"—Katherine again eyed Steve, though tried not to look too concerned—"could we maybe...?"

Steve got her hint. "I'll be inside when you folks are ready." He went in and closed the door behind him.

"All right, what are you babbling about?" Jordan asked.

"I found two more bodies," Katherine whispered.

"What do you mean 'two more bodies'?"

"Just like your great-whatever grandmother Gloria. Probably your great uncle Reginald and great-grandfather Vernon."

"In the mansion?"

"Yes."

"What were they doing there? Playing *Mario Kart*?"

She ignored his, well, she couldn't call it a joke, but whatever it was supposed to be, she ignored it. "Well, that's what I'd kinda like to talk to you about."

"Okay?"

"Jordan, they were buried in the basement."

"What, like in the dirt and gravel?"

"Not exactly." She eyed the front doors to make sure that Steve had, in fact, closed them behind him. It looked like he had. "They were buried in special tombs built for them."

"In the mansion?"

"Yeah."

"Why weren't they buried in the family cemetery?" He cast a look to his right, in the cemetery's direction.

"I don't know. Jordan, that's what I'm saying. Something really weird is going on with your family—*was* going on. Maybe something dangerous. I think we should figure out what it was before we do anything else. Like, host a Halloween party here."

He looked both annoyed and relieved. "Oh, that's what this is about!"

"What?"

"You've always hated the idea of the Halloween event!"

"No, I don't hate it. I just—"

"Sure you do. Ever since I first mentioned it, you've resisted it."

"That was only because I didn't think you could have the place ready in time to host a bunch of, as you said, guests, influencers, and DJ."

"*I'm* the DJ!"

"Yeah, I know, but you'd still have to set up. Lights, generators, your equipment."

"That's why we're here. For the lights and electricity."

"I know, but we should really figure out what to do about the basement." She whispered, "Your dead family."

"Look, Kat, I appreciate your concern, but can we talk about this later? We've already made Steven wait twice now."

"Okay, but we need to—"

"Of course. Later." He turned away from her, opened the right door, and headed in. "Sorry about that, Steven."

"Hey, no problem," Steve said from inside. "Just takin' in the place."

Katherine walked in after them. *I mean, I told him. Maybe I shouldn't worry about it anymore.*

Inside, she found Steve with a flashlight out, inspecting every inch of the entryway hall's walls, staircase, and twin statues, Artemis and Apollo. Jordan walked up next to him, and while not seeming nearly as impressed, he did take a moment to look the walls up and down.

"An old lumber family, your folks?" Steve asked Jordan.

"No, my parents were involved mostly in charities."

"No, your folks, your family, your kin."

"Oh. Right. Them. Yeah. Sure. I think so."

*I might need to interject. Seems like Jordan's about three seconds away from smacking Steve upside the head like a lord to his servant.* "So did we need to, uh...?"

Steve seemed to suddenly realize why they were all there. "Right! So, uh, the basement?"

Jordan faced Katherine with a stern expression that seemed to say "Do *not* mention my dead family's bodies." "Kat? The basement?"

Steve also faced her, looking relieved that someone around here had some clue what was going on.

"Um, how would I know?" Katherine asked.

"Um, because you've been here a bunch of times," Jordan said.

"It's your house."

"And as I told you before, I haven't been inside here since I was a kid."

# THE POSSESSION OF BLACKSTONE MANSION

Likely picking up on the rising tensions, Steve inserted himself between them without violating either one's personal space. "It's not a problem, folks. All we gotta do is find it."

*I dunno that that's such a good idea, Steve.* "Uh, does the fuse box or whatever, does it have to be in the basement?"

"No, not at all. Traditional, but not mandatory."

"So if you found one or could install one somewhere around here"—Katherine indicated the entire entryway hall—"that'd be cool?"

"Yeah, we can install it anywhere. I just figured you folks'd wanna use whatever they already had."

"I doubt they had anything," Jordan scoffed.

"How would we find out?" Katherine asked.

"Unless you have a plan that shows where they installed it, we'd have to, well, check the ground floor," Steve said.

"Wait. You mean the entire ground floor?" Jordan asked.

"A simple walk around the perimeter should show us what we need to know."

Satisfied that they wouldn't wander around aimlessly in the dark inside, Katherine asked Jordan, "Well, what are we waiting for?" She led them outside.

The three walked along the mansion's eastern perimeter. She'd picked this direction hoping they'd find whatever box Steve was looking for before he had a chance to spot the cemetery. Not that the existence of a family cemetery on the property was so beyond the pale, but she didn't want him to ask Jordan any questions.

Along the way, she started in on her own questions to Steve, just to keep them all talking. "So, what are we looking for, exactly?"

"Oh, it'll be a box about yay high." Steve put his hands on top of and bottom of an invisible box about three feet high. "About yay wide." He put his hands on the sides of the invisible box about four feet wide. "Usually gray, though I've seen orange, green. It'll be connected to at least one wire that either goes up or down and at least another that heads inside."

"Fascinating," Jordan snorted.

"Will it, you know, still work?" Katherine asked.

"Oh, that depends. Some of this old equipment goes kaput in only a few short years. Some lasts forever." He looked up the side of the wall. "Lookin' like your family spared no expense on anything, so I'm guessing the box is probably just fine. The wire, on the other hand..."

Jordan halted. "What do you mean, the wire?"

"Well, if they got connected to the grid with overhanging wire, you know, with those poles that run along the street—"

"Telephone poles, yes," Jordan cut him off.

"Then it's probably okay, so long as a storm or high winds never blew 'em down in the last—How old you say this place was?"

"I didn't," Jordan stated plainly.

"It's over a century," Katherine answered.

Steve nodded. "If they did underground wiring, obviously no wind's gonna get at it, but after so long, almost certainly corroded. And I hate to inform you, Mr. Blackstone, but I didn't see no poles."

"Fantastic." Jordan rolled his eyes and kept walking.

Steve and Katherine followed. They turned the first corner.

"So, Steve," Katherine said, "assuming it is underground wiring and maybe a functioning box, how long would that take to repair or upgrade?"

Jordan shot her a look, likely not at all appreciating her insinuation that such work couldn't possibly be done in time for his little Halloween shindig.

"Ooh, I mean"—Steve paused to consider the full weight of her question—"fixing, or worse, replacing the box, that'd take at least a few days."

Jordan rolled his eyes at the woods. "Great."

"I'm afraid it gets worse, Mr. Blackstone."

"Lay it on me."

"Well, even assuming the best-case scenario with the fuse box, like I say, from what I've seen, there aren't any poles, which means all the work's underground. I think you're looking at complete re-installation on that."

Jordan looked like he was struggling to remain calm. "Are you telling me that in order to do *anything* with this"—he shook a stern finger at the mansion—"crumbling monstrosity, I'll have to pay for *all* the underground wiring to be replaced?"

Steve looked like he was trying to paint this whole situation in the best possible light... and about to utterly fail. "Yes, Mr. Blackstone, that might very well be the case."

"Might very well be or *will* be?" Jordan practically shouted.

Katherine got between him and Steve. "Let's all take a breath."

"What do you gotta breathe for?" Jordan asked. "You're not paying for this stuff!"

"Jordan? Deep breath," Katherine instructed.

Jordan did as he was told.

"I wonder, Steve, given the mansion's age and status in the community, having been built by the town's founders, I wonder if perhaps the state would look on it as, say, a historical landmark. And perhaps the Blackstone family foundation might come up with an arrangement in which the cost of upgrading the house's connection to the electrical grid were considered a state investment into a historical prop-

# THE POSSESSION OF BLACKSTONE MANSION

erty which the state"—Katherine smiled at Jordan, driving it home—"would find advantageous to keep up, as, say, a tourist attraction, museum, whatever."

Steve looked like he knew what she was suggesting, but didn't at all want to get involved. "Uh, that question, Kat, sounds like something best left to Mr. Blackstone's attorneys. What I will say, though, is yes, the wiring from the house to the grid will almost certainly need to be replaced."

"Son of a..." Jordan grumbled mostly to himself, but Katherine and Steve could definitely hear.

"Shall we?" Katherine gestured for them to continue around the house.

"'Course." Steve led the way.

Jordan said nothing and followed.

They soon turned the second corner.

"So once any box is upgraded or replaced and once any wiring is replaced, then Mr. Blackstone will be able to light this baby right up, won't he?" Katherine asked.

"With neon Christmas lights if he wants!" Steve exclaimed.

"'Tis the season," Jordan said.

"'Course that'd be awfully high electricity consumption if he—if you covered the whole house, Mr. Blackstone."

"I'd imagine so."

"Oh! There she is!" Steve pointed to a gray box attached to the wall of the north tower a few feet above the ground.

They eagerly walked a little faster to the fuse box.

As they approached, Steve motioned for Katherine and Jordan to stay back. "For your safety. Might be live, might be exposed wire, might be…"

"We got it," Jordan said.

Steve put on a pair of safety gloves. He poked around the box's door latch.

Katherine couldn't tell whether it was locked or stuck or just sticky.

"Yeah, you're definitely gonna have to get this replaced," Steve confirmed.

"All right," Jordan lamented.

"At least now we know," Katherine reassured.

*Snap!* They heard metal pop open, but it sounded to Katherine like it had cracked in half.

"What in the hell?" Steve asked.

"What is it?" Jordan asked.

Steve stepped away from the open box. Inside, someone had attacked the interior with a heavy, sharp implement like an ax or shovel. Everything was smashed. All wires were cut. This had been the work of no storm or fallen tree. Someone had done this.

Intentionally.

## 21

Katherine and Jordan were back at the gate, watching Steve pull away in his PGE van. Jordan had just gotten an estimate from Steve of time and cost for repairs to get everything back up and running.

It was a lot.

"Guess I'll give my lawyers a call," Jordan remarked.

Katherine desperately did not want to ask him about his proposed Halloween event, and possibly request that he hold off till next year, since she was sure he'd flip his lid. At the same time, she knew that with the recent discovery of more bodies in the house, there was now the need to alert the police about them. To do so would shut down his event. To not do so was illegal.

Then she was also concerned that if he decided that the show must go on, that such a rowdy get-together would arouse the Blackstone family spirits in ways they couldn't predict.

"Jordan, that fuse box." She didn't know what else to say about the fact that someone had intentionally destroyed the box's wires and other internal components.

"Yeah."

"What is going on here? The bodies in the basement. Who would've murdered your family? What stories are there? What are you not telling me?"

"You honestly think if there were something to tell, I wouldn't tell you?" He pointed back up at the mansion. "Kat, until only a few weeks ago, I hadn't given this place, or whatever it was hiding, a single thought for decades."

"Fine, but you have to admit, it's all pretty disturbing."

"Absolutely."

"Beyond just adding spice to ad copy for Halloween."

"I *knew* you weren't gonna let that go!"

"You're talking about having people here, real people, with friggin' dead people!"

"If they don't know..."

"You were going on about how your dead relatives would help sell the event!"

"Sure, the *idea* of them, not the actual bodies."

"But that's what's actually there! We have to tell the police!"

"*We* don't have to do anything. I'm not till after the party. And you're not because I'm telling you not to."

"Jordan, I can't just—"

"Check our contract."

She sighed, positive that even if there weren't some clause specifically telling her not to talk to the police about discovered bodies in the basement, that he'd sic his lawyers on her, anyway. That would take time and money, the bulk of hers which was currently coming from him. "Fine. I promise I won't alert the police."

"Excellent."

"But only till after your event."

"Fine by me."

He started for his car. She stood there for a second, feeling frustrated and stuck, and hating both.

"Need a ride?" he asked.

*And of course I'm literally stuck out here without him.* "Yeah. Thanks." She followed him to his car.

They were silent all the way back to her place. The closer they got, the more the dread crept up on her. As much as she liked her apartment, it had been so tainted ever since she'd brought back that pendant. *And yet, I still keep it.*

He parked right in front. "Remember, Kat, wealthy matron."

"What?" She was still distracted by the possibility of more Vernon encounters at her place.

# AUGUSTINE PIERCE

"Your costume." Jordan referred to her need to dress up for his event. "Oh, and please, invite your boyfriend. He'll have a blast."

"No problem." She got out. She meant it literally. There would be no problem. She could find a costume and wear it. She could ask Kirk to come with her. But the fact was, she didn't want Kirk around Jordan. She was afraid Jordan might pick on him or something worse, like coerce Kirk to move his DJ equipment in and out.

Entering her apartment, she took out her phone and texted Kirk, mostly because she actually needed to communicate Jordan's costume request before she forgot, but also so she could distract herself from Vernon, possibly hiding around a corner.

> Hey, what are you doing Halloween night?

---

Katherine's Uber dropped her right outside the auto body shop where AAA had sent her car. As much as she didn't love dealing with mechanics, she even more didn't love how she'd depended on Kirk, Uber, and, worst of all, Jordan these last few days.

She walked in, greeted the receptionist, and went through the necessary pleasantries and forms. She then sat and waited for close to ten minutes for the mechanic to come get her.

After looking over a fashion magazine from several months ago, she heard a gruff, but friendly, male voice address her.

"Ms. Norrington?" the mechanic asked.

She looked up to find a short, balding man in coveralls. "That's me."

"We got you all ready if you'd like to follow me."

"Great." She set down the magazine, stood, and followed him.

He led her to the garage entrance, where her car sat good as new. She was impressed. It looked like it had never received a single scratch. *Probably just replaced everything.*

"Damage was pretty extensive," the mechanic said.

"Uh-huh?"

"Yeah, all along this side." He moved his hand across the side of the car.

*Yeah, dude, I remember. I was there.* "Right."

"Were you cut off or something? Side swiped?"

"No. Not as insidious as that."

He looked really confused. She didn't know whether it was because of the situation that had gotten her here or her use of the word insidious.

She indulged his curiosity. "Kinda hit a tree."

He looked even more confused. "Didn't see it comin'?"

"Not exactly." *'Cause a frickin' ghost invaded my back seat!*

"Well, be careful out there. Never know who's next to you."

*Or sitting right behind you.* "Yeah. Thanks."

He handed her the keys. "You have yourself a good day, Ms. Norrington."

"Thank you. You too." She got in and drove off.

---

Katherine sat on her sofa, staring at her purse. Despite the trouble that it had almost certainly caused her, she was so tempted to take out that pendant and study it more. Touch it more. Admire it more.

She caved, opening her purse, and taking out the pendant.

She held it up to the light coming in from her living room windows. She let her eyes trace its lines. *So pretty.* She relaxed her arms, lowering it to her lap. "What? It's not pretty! It's tacky if it's anything. Black and platinum?"

She set it on the coffee table. *Yet I can't stop looking at it. Like a fiery car crash. I know I shouldn't, but...* "And why so much fuss over this symbol?" She thought about the fact that the very structure of Blackstone mansion had been built as a direct representation of

# THE POSSESSION OF BLACKSTONE MANSION

the pendant's shape. Right down to its circles being the literal towers.

She picked up the pendant, stuffed it in her purse, and shoved it to the end of the sofa.

Something was nagging at the back of her head. Something she was forgetting. She leapt to her feet. "Leeyah!"

---

As Katherine pulled up to her store, she saw Aleeyah standing outside. Aleeyah was strikingly attractive with her long, styled hair, supermodel face, and gray coat. While she wore a bright smile that was so well rehearsed, most people didn't notice how rehearsed it was, Katherine could tell. *Great, Kat, second time in, like, a month that you've made Leeyah wait.* The previous time had been weeks ago when Katherine had requested Aleeyah fly out from New York to see Vernon's firearms collection, when Katherine had then gotten into a scuffle with her landlord, had been forced to spend the night at Blackstone's one motel, and so had completely forgotten that Aleeyah and other contacts were showing up to bid over Vernon's collection. The incident had been embarrassing.

Katherine pulled up and jumped out. "'Afternoon!"

She and Aleeyah gave each other a quick greeting kiss.

"You are a hard woman to find, Ms. Norrington!" Aleeyah said with good cheer, but there was a definite edge to her voice.

"Yeah, it's been a nuts few days."

"Do tell, do tell!"

"Eh, I don't wanna bore you with the trifles." Katherine opened the front door and held it wide for her. "No Miles or Chase? Anybody else?"

Aleeyah shrugged. "They snooze..." She then feasted her eyes on the mansion's riches. "Darling, you were not kidding! Look at this!" She regarded Katherine as if she'd never seen any of it before.

"Right?"

"I mean, where to even begin?"

"So, the back half is from the music room. Or rather, a music room. There may be more."

Aleeyah chuckled at the notion of the possibility of so many more pieces. "The harpsichord."

"Right."

"You know, one of my clients, his favorite film, absolute favorite, is *Amadeus*."

"The director's cut?"

"Is there any other?"

Katherine grinned. "Front half, the smoking room."

"Or perhaps *a* smoking room?"

"If you wanted to take a closer look."

"I don't mind if I do." Aleeyah entered. Inside, she carefully stepped around various pieces, inching her way toward the back. "Darling, this is some truly impressive... stuff!"

"Yeah."

"And you said all from one family?"

"Yep. Old lumber family. I think one of the early ones to the state."

"So much history."

Katherine wondered if now was the time to bring up all the murderous conspiracy. "You don't know the half of it."

"Oh?" Aleeyah faced her.

"So the Blackstones' favorite hobbies were hunting, horses, murdering their kids' fiancées, and possibly each other."

"Oh my God! Do tell, do tell!"

Katherine relayed the stories of Eileen, Gloria, Reginald, and Vernon, though left out details such as the tombs.

"Katherine, that is incredible!" Aleeyah exclaimed. "And, uh, the property's current owner can verify all this?"

"Him and county law enforcement."

"I'm going to have to jump on the phone. I can think of at least three who'd be deeply interested."

Katherine nodded, trying hard not to look too eager.

Aleeyah excused herself, hiked back to the entrance, then excused herself again to make some calls.

"Don't take too long, Leeyah. I've got other lines dangling!" Katherine warned.

Aleeyah held up a finger as she poked around on her phone. "You naughty minx. Don't you dare reel any of those in until I've had my chance."

Katherine grinned and shrugged as if to say "Better hurry."

Aleeyah stepped away to make her calls.

Katherine sent her own texts to other contacts. She got responses immediately. Everything from...

> Don't let her take it all before I get out there

...to...

> If Leeyah presses one key on that harpsichord before I get my chance, I'll never speak to you again!

Within a few minutes of Katherine's and Aleeyah's calls and texts, Miles, the tall, handsome Brit, Chase, the short Angelino, and two others had arrived. They all got down to brass tacks. So much so that now Katherine was having to fend off the potential buyers momentarily as Jordan and his legal team got involved.

# THE POSSESSION OF BLACKSTONE MANSION

"Wait, so this is all for just the music room?" Jordan asked.

"So far, yes," Katherine said.

"Darling, how many family members were murdered?" Aleeyah asked.

"Three, but also Reginald's fiancée."

"Which one was Reginald?"

"The older brother. Heir to the fortune before he died."

"Of a gunshot wound?"

"Well, probably more from the blood asphyxiation than the actual wound."

"So juicy!"

"What size was the exit wound?" Chase asked.

"I didn't measure it, Chase," Katherine said.

"Ballpark?"

"Why does it matter?"

"Dude wants to know."

"Tell him size of a quarter."

"Huh." Chase sounded very disappointed.

"Silver dollar!"

"Ah! And the harpsichord? Condition?"

"Perfect!"

"You're not selling that incredible instrument to some movie mogul, are you?" Miles asked.

"Not yet, but..."

"Don't you dare!" Aleeyah ordered.

"So the harpsichord's gonna be in a movie?" Jordan asked.

"I dunno," Katherine said. "I doubt it. Probably just gonna keep it in his private collection."

"Who is this again?"

"Produced those movies about fast cars and hot women?"

"Isn't that, like, all of them?"

An hour later, Jordan had sold the contents of his family's music room to Aleeyah for two million dollars. Katherine had been right. With the first mention of his family's murderous history, prices just kept going up.

After hanging up with a delighted Jordan, Katherine said her goodbyes to Aleeyah, Miles, Chase, and the others, and they agreed to meet the following afternoon to take care of the contents of the smoking room.

Katherine returned to her apartment. She retired to her bedroom, where she planned to chill with her laptop resting on her stomach playing a documentary when her phone *buzzed*. Turning to reach for it, her laptop slid off and nearly fell on the floor. She grabbed it in time and, even more luckily, was able to set it aside and get to her phone before the caller hung up.

She saw it was Kirk and answered with an instant rush of delight. "Hey!"

"Hey, you."

"Get my text?"

"Halloween party?"

"Yep, but only if you wanna go."

"Yeah. I mean, why not? Could be fun. Is this an apple-bobbing sort of affair?"

She rolled her eyes. "No idea. Jordan's throwing it at the mansion. I expect it'll be him spinning his 'tunes'"—she held up air quotes with her free hand—"and not a whole lot else."

"Still."

"Still indeed. So he's tasked me with getting myself a period costume."

"Oh?"

"Yeah. I guess he really wants to play up the mansion's history. Or the history of the mansion when it was abandoned."

"I mean, why not? The nineteen twenties are plenty creepy."

"Right? I was wondering if you'd mind accompanying me on acquiring said costume. Oh, and sounds like he wants you to dress up too."

"I am so down."

She smiled. "Well, you don't have to be if you don't wanna."

"No, seriously. I don't even remember the last time I went to a Halloween party."

"Really?"

"Yeah, I think my pals all sorta outgrew the whole thing when they discovered girls."

"So why didn't you?"

"Never discovered girls."

"Oh please."

"Okay, one or two."

"So now the big question is, where's the nearest Spirit Halloween 'cause I'm damn sure there isn't one down the street."

"I'll google it. Ooh, looks like the nearest one is in Oregon City."

"Right by your bowling alley?"

"Not quite, but it's a small town."

"How about I swing by, we make the hike, I grab some flapper dress, you whatever, we go back to your place, you kick me out tomorrow morning?"

"Sounds like a plan. Except for the kicking."

"Soft nudging."

He laughed. "See you in a bit."

---

The drive out to Oregon City was peaceful. Kirk complained a little about his job, how his coworker Annie had recently grown much more distant, much colder toward him. Katherine knew the last bit was almost certainly her fault since she'd rather handily dressed Annie down, specifically accusing her of being in love with Kirk, which Katherine was sure she was, but she hadn't anticipated Annie taking it out on him.

Kirk wondered whether car rental was really his future. While he had no illusions about becoming the drummer for a world-famous rock band, he wasn't sure that he wanted to spend the rest of his life handing car keys to tourists.

They arrived at Spirit Halloween, a pop-up chain Halloween costume store that boasted not only its cheap and kitschy sign, but a blow-up mummy and black cat flanking the entrance.

Kirk chuckled as they entered. "Man, I haven't been to one of these things in years."

"Me neither."

They surveyed the inventory. There were costumes, wall hangings, and various glow-in-the-dark knick-knacks. She zeroed in on the women's section. She found sexy nurses, sexy witches, and sexy sorceresses. *Why is it always sexy? What, men can't be sexy zombies or werewolves?*

She laughed when she found the only costume that was specific to her period. "Of course."

"Ha!" he laughed.

She held up a flapper outfit. "Did I not call it?"

"You sure did."

"So, now you."

"Man, where do we even start? Want me to match?"

"I mean, not necessarily. I guess if we can."

They wandered over to the men's section. They found gladiators, grim reapers, and evil clowns.

"Oh lookie here." He smiled lecherously as he wrapped his fingers around a nineteen twenties gangster complete with pinstripe suit and Tommy gun.

"Oh no."

"Oh yes."

"It's so..."

"Perfect?"

"Flapper and gangster? Seriously?"

"Peanut butter and chocolate. And probably our only option."

"All right. Let's get 'em."

They brought their selections to the cashier, a bored-looking guy not a day over twenty.

"So what happened with Jordan?" Kirk asked.

"Hm?" Katherine asked. *No, Kirk, let's not get into this now.*

"Bag?" the cashier asked.

"Yeah. Thanks."

"The, uh"—Kirk whispered—"bodies?" He threw the cashier a quick glance to make sure he wasn't paying attention.

He wasn't. He dug a bag out from under the counter and scanned the costumes.

*Seriously, Kirk? You're asking me about century-plus-old murdered dead bodies while we're paying for our Halloween costumes?* "Um, didn't really come up." *Oh no. That's hardly plausible.*

"Didn't...?" Kirk asked.

The cashier waited for them. He glanced over at the total amount for the costumes.

Katherine took out her card.

"No, Kat, I can get this." Kirk took out his wallet.

"No, no, I invited." *At least now we're haggling over this and not what Jordan and I talked about.*

"No, come on. You're doing me a favor by taking me out to a party." Kirk attempted to hand over his card.

The cashier looked confused. His eyes bounced between the two, likely just wanting them to make up their minds.

Katherine placed a hand over Kirk's card. "Your money's no good here." She gave the cashier her card.

"You sure?" Kirk asked.

"Yep."

"But I make all that car-rental cheddar."

The cashier handed back Katherine her card.

"Too late. Already done." She grinned as she accepted the bagged costumes.

As they headed out to the car, Kirk picked up the Jordan thread all over again. "So you never mentioned the bodies to Jordan?"

She waited as he unlocked the doors. Getting in, she crafted her words carefully. "We discussed it briefly."

He closed his door and started the car. "So it did come up?"

"Yeah, I just... The guy in there. Didn't wanna..."

"Right. So what did Jordan say?"

"You're not gonna believe it or like it."

"Okay?"

"He kinda didn't care."

"What do you mean?"

"He's been obsessed with this whole Halloween-party idea ever since he first dreamed it up. He wants it to go on, doesn't want anything to get in the way, so he ordered me not to pursue it."

"Ordered you?"

"Yes."

"Can he even do that?"

"Apparently, my contract contains some clause or other that covers it, yes."

"You didn't have an attorney look at it?"

"I did not."

"Why not?"

"Because I didn't, Kirk. I was desperate at the time and didn't wanna drag out negotiations."

"Sorry."

"No, it's fine. It's a perfectly reasonable question."

"So you're not telling the police about the bodies you found?"

"I am not. For now."

"So wait, we and he and whoever else comes to this thing, we're gonna be partying over two dead bodies?"

"Assuming what we'll be doing can be called partying, yes."

"That's, like, weird."

"Yes it is."

"I mean, Kat, that's, like, really weird."

"Is it any weirder than midnight projections of *Night of the Living Dead* in cemeteries?"

"What in cemeteries?"

"You know, people gather in cemeteries at night and watch films projected on monuments or whatever. Usually horror films like *Night*."

"I mean, I guess I've heard of it, but I've never done it."

It again delighted her that they weren't directly talking about the bodies in Jordan's basement. "We should go! Probably too late this year, but we should totally go."

"Um, yeah, maybe. So if you and Jordan aren't telling the police about bodies buried in the bottom of his mansion because of this party, when are you telling them?"

"I presume after the party."

"You presume?"

"We didn't exactly have a detailed conversation about it, no."

"Kat, bodies, the police."

"Kirk, I don't know what you want me to do. The man's basically my only source of income. In the last few weeks, he's threatened me with legal action no fewer than three times. He did when I even suggested telling the police. So as far as I can tell, he holds all the strings."

"Maybe you shouldn't work for him."

"Maybe not, but right now, I am."

Kirk nodded and with that, the conversation ended. Luckily, they only had another few minutes before they reached his place.

As they pulled over, she placed her hand on his before he let go of the steering wheel. "I know it got a little tense back there, so if you don't want me to stay, I can go."

"No, I'd love you to stay. I'm just concerned, is all."

"I know. That's very sweet." She gave him a quick kiss.

They headed in and got to the rest of their evening, which consisted mainly of a simple spaghetti dinner, washing up, trying on their costumes, lots of laughter over that, and finally bed time.

## 22

Katherine awoke to the sound of Kirk stomping around as he attempted to put on his pants.

"'Morning," she greeted.

"Good morning."

"How'd you sleep?"

"Great after..." He grinned like a boy who'd been caught with his hand in the cookie jar.

She chuckled. "Yeah. So I was thinking..."

"Always a terrible sign."

"I don't want you to think me too forward."

He pointed to her clothes tossed about the room.

"Not just about sex," she said. "Fact is, ever since, well, everything, but especially being locked in that tomb, I was kinda wondering..."

"Yeah. Of course."

"You don't know what I was gonna ask."

"If you can stay."

"Oh okay, yeah, that was what I was gonna ask."

"So yeah. Of course."

# THE POSSESSION OF BLACKSTONE MANSION

"Only for a few days. Till after the party. After I... I dunno, take care of whatever it is the remaining Blackstone family spirits want."

"And you report their bodies to the police."

*Was hoping you'd forgotten about that.* "Right. Of course. I'll drop by my place today, get my laptop, clothes, toiletries. I promise I'll stay outta your way, outta your space."

He finished getting dressed. "It's okay, Kat. You can stay as long as you want."

"Come here."

"I gotta go." But he joined her by the bed.

She pulled him down. "Gimme a kiss."

They kissed.

"Have some coffee," he said.

"I will. Thanks."

"See you tonight." He left.

She got dressed and showered, then headed out to her place. Now that he'd agreed to let her stay with him, being at her apartment didn't freak her out quite so much. In fact, the existence of an option made her feel empowered.

Entering her living room, she located her carry-on bag, the only one she arrived with in Blackstone all those weeks ago. She threw in clothes, toiletries, and her laptop, and hurried out the door.

She sat in her car in her store's parking lot, unsure what to do next. She had a few hours till sales began today. She eyed the front door, the memory of Vernon's appearance inside still fresh. She stared straight ahead and decided. "Screw this."

---

Katherine sat in Blackstone's diner, nursing the latest cup of cocoa. She'd had Wendy keep them coming for what seemed like hours now, even though it was only a few minutes. Checking the time, she saw it was only 9:30. She lifted the cup to her lips.

A terrible stench wafted into her nostrils. "What the...?" She felt an intense chill on the left side of her body. "Come on," she said to herself as she lowered her cup to the counter.

She took an unsteady breath as she let her eyes drift to the left. Intense darkness invaded her peripheral vision. She recognized the edge of bone, the texture of flesh.

She launched to her feet and marched around the counter to the cadaverous form. Her mouth opened before she'd taken a second to think about what she'd say. A flurry of curses spilled out. "The stupid party wasn't my idea! I tried to talk Jordan out of it! Go haunt him! Leave me alone!" She followed up with more cursing.

# THE POSSESSION OF BLACKSTONE MANSION

A hand squeezed her left shoulder. She shouted and faced the hand's owner.

Wendy stared at her with deep concern. "Kat?"

"What?" Katherine demanded. She saw who had been in front of her this whole time. It was Mr. Beavers—she didn't know his actual name—a man wearing a Beavers cap, who weeks ago had been the first to inform her all about Blackstone mansion.

His eyes were wide with fright, most likely at the verbal assault she'd just lobbed at him.

"I'm sorry. I—I dunno what—I—I'm sorry," Katherine said.

"Hon, maybe it's time for a walk?" Wendy asked, but she was really insisting.

"A walk." Katherine spotted her empty cocoa mug on the counter. "My bill."

"On the house," Wendy insisted again, and eased her out of the diner.

Outside, Katherine wandered onto the town square and found her usual bench. She sat and heaved an enormous sigh as she took in the mountain's beauty. *I'm losing my goddamn mind!* Before she knew it, drowsiness overwhelmed her. *Just gonna...* She rested her head on her folded arms on the back of the bench. That turned out to be severely uncomfortable, so she full-on laid down on the bench's seat. Before she knew it, she was out.

## AUGUSTINE PIERCE

"Ma'am?" a familiar male voice asked Katherine. "Ma'am? Can you sit up, please?"

Katherine opened her eyes. She was still sprawled out on the park bench. She looked up. It was the sheriff. The one who had intervened when her previous landlord and current insurance policy holder, Drew, had kicked her out of his house. The sheriff had sympathized with her, but ultimately been forced to take Drew's side.

"Oh, hey. It's you," she said.

"Ma'am?"

"No. Nothing. How long've I been out?"

"I don't know, ma'am, but we've received some complaints."

"Complaints? What?"

"Your napping here. Vagrancy."

"What? Are you serious?"

"'Fraid so, ma'am."

"I can't take a nap on a public bench?"

"We've had complaints."

"So you said." She scanned the square and surrounding buildings to see if she could catch the snitch.

She found no one.

# THE POSSESSION OF BLACKSTONE MANSION

*Probably hiding in their house or store, staring at me right now.* She gave her field of vision one more quick glance. *Nope. Nobody. Wait. Who's that?*

All the way at the other end of the square, a very tall, thin man stood right at the corner of a building. His skin was so pale he looked days dead. She couldn't tell whether it was his natural color or a mask or makeup. *Why would anyone wear that shade of makeup?* His skin was so smooth of any wrinkle or blemish, she couldn't tell his age. Anywhere between fifty and eighty. He wore a black hat with a thick wide rim, like a blend between a bowler and a traditional Amish hat. He also wore fiercely black glasses, so dark she saw no hint of eyes behind them. A black trench coat cascaded down his whole body, so far it even covered his shoes. *Is he...? Is he looking at me?*

"Ma'am, I'm gonna have to ask you to get up," the sheriff said.

"Yeah." She was still so distracted by the man in black, she wasn't quite registering the sheriff. She stood and brushed herself off.

"You have a place you can go?"

She gave him her full attention. *No.* "Yeah, I'll get outta your hair."

"Sorry about this, ma'am."

"No, it's fine. Just doing your job."

As she walked toward her car, she threw that one corner a quick glance.

The man in black was gone.

She got in her car and drove back to her store. Even though the time said 12:48, Aleeyah was already there. *God, I just wanna crash at Kirk's place.*

She got out of her car and tried to muster up some enthusiasm for Aleeyah. "Hey."

"Happy Wednesday! So, to the smoking room?"

"Yeah." Katherine dug out her store keys. "Earliest bird again?"

"Seems so—Oh my God, what is that?" Aleeyah pointed to Katherine's open purse.

"What's what?"

"That!" Aleeyah pointed insistently.

Katherine realized it was the pendant, sitting on top of everything else in her purse, that had so seized Aleeyah's eye. "Nothing."

"What do you mean, nothing?"

"It's just a... piece of jewelry."

"Is it from the mansion?"

Katherine desperately did not want to answer that question, but felt she had no choice. "It's not part of the smoking room."

"But it is from the mansion?"

"Leeyah, it's nothing. Hardly worth anything."

"Isn't that platinum?" Aleeyah referred to the shining stripe that ran down the middle of each of the pendant's bars.

"Yes."

"Well, I'd say that's worth something."

"It's not." Katherine held her purse against her stomach.

"Why won't you show me?" Aleeyah's tone was shifting from polite excitement to irritation.

"Because it's just this trinket! This piece of crap that I found in some dusty back room!"

Aleeyah's eyes lit up. "What, like a private study?"

"Yes! I mean, no! Just a boring, old, dusty room!"

"Family murders and now a piece of twisted old jewelry from a private study? One hundred!"

"It's not for sale."

"Two hundred!"

"Leeyah, I'm serious. It's not part of a room, not part of a collection, not for sale."

Aleeyah looked severely confused. "I don't understand. You're handling the estate."

"Yes."

"That piece is part of the estate." Aleeyah pointed to Katherine's purse.

"Yes. I mean, no. It is, but—"

"Then I imagine it's for sale."

"Leeyah, please."

"Why don't you want to sell it to me? Did the owner give you some arbitrary mandate?"

"No, he didn't."

"What's his name again?"

"Jordan."

"Well, then, I'm guessing Mr. Jordan Blackstone would be perfectly willing to take some money and I can think of at least a dozen people who'd love to give it to him." She took out her phone and started scrolling numbers.

Katherine snatched her phone.

Aleeyah's tone grew deadly serious. "Katherine? Kindly remove your hand from my phone."

Katherine released her phone and stepped back. "You know what? Fine. Call him. I don't care." She jumped back into her car.

"Kat, where are you going? We're still in the middle of"—Aleeyah pointed to the store—"everything!"

Katherine ignored her. She fired up her car and drove straight to Kirk's place.

"Kat?" Kirk knocked on glass.

Katherine opened her eyes. *Again?* She looked to her left. She saw a very concerned-looking Kirk standing right next to her window. "Oh,

# THE POSSESSION OF BLACKSTONE MANSION

hey." She peered down at her phone. The screen was off. She pressed the home button. It turned on and showed her it was 5:34. *What happened? Got into a tiff with Leeyah, came over here, played some* Fruit Ninja, *and...*

"What you doin' passed out in your car?"

"Uh, nothing. Just, uh, wanted to drop by early."

"Even though I wasn't gonna be here?"

"Yeah, I mean... Yeah."

He smiled. "Well, why don't you come in?"

"Sounds like a grand idea."

She followed him inside. *Better smooth things over with Leeyah. And everyone else. Tomorrow. Or whenever. Right now, literally anything else.*

## 23

Katherine texted Aleeyah and the others the next morning apologizing for her odd behavior and blaming the whole thing on a lack of sleep, which was partially true, and not feeling well lately.

Aleeyah was the most forgiving, wishing Katherine well, and informing her she was eager to resume their negotiations over the antiques once Katherine was ready. Miles was terse with a simple...

> No prob, love.

Chase was grumpier with some complaint about having flown all the way up from LA.

With Kirk gone for the day, she felt stifled. She'd excused herself from further antique-related work, so she had no need to go to her store. She'd freaked out at the diner, so didn't want to show her face there. She no longer felt welcome in her own apartment, so she didn't go there either. She decided just to stay at Kirk's, and do what little research she could into the mansion's various curiosities, from its secret tombs to its strange floor plan, to the origins of the pendant's symbol.

Before she got started, she triple checked every corner of Kirk's apartment to make sure there were no signs of hiding spirits. She knew she couldn't stop them from showing up, but she wanted to have a jump start. Despite her effort, she spied no moving shadow, felt no chill. Satisfied that at least for now no one would bother her, she got down to business.

After several hours of diving headfirst into various internet rabbit holes, she'd come up with nothing. Absolutely nothing.

At last, the time arrived, and she eagerly awaited Kirk outside.

He walked up. "Hey!"

"Happy Halloween."

"To you too."

They kissed, and he opened the building's door. "Ready?" he asked.

"Not until I get that flapper outfit on."

They went inside, had dinner, and got ready with their costumes. They each posed in front of the mirror several times, then together a bunch. They took a dozen pictures. It was like they were hanging out in a vintage photo booth, without the tight, cumbersome space of an actual photo booth.

Heading out, he kept fussing with his gangster suit, pulling on the sleeves, and lining up the shoulder pads.

"Stop fidgeting," she said.

"I'm not fidgeting."

"You are." She stopped and did one final once-over of his costume.

"I look ridiculous, don't I?" He sounded like he was desperate for the answer to be no.

"Of course you do!" She smiled. "But so do I."

"Let's do this."

"Yeah. Let's." She hooked her arm around his until they got to her car.

Getting in, they both sighed.

"Is this, like, really weird?" he asked.

"What? That we're headed out to a technically still-abandoned and haunted mansion to dance the night away directly above two dead bodies?"

"Yeah. That."

"Another day at the office."

"I guess."

She got them going, and they listened to cheesy Halloween standards all the way to the mansion.

Nearing the gate, they found a veritable auto graveyard of parked cars, two rows all the way down the road to its first turn back to town, close to a mile away. Whatever Jordan had done to attract last-minute attention to this event, it had worked.

# THE POSSESSION OF BLACKSTONE MANSION

On getting out of the car, Katherine noticed one group of early twentysomethings off to the side smoking, and another group on their phones. *Right, no signal on the property.* She guessed that not only were those of the second group updating social feeds, but since Jordan had mentioned it, a number of them were probably influencers spreading the word.

In front of them, two giant lights towered over the sides of the gate's doors. They provided blinding illumination for a myriad of branded posters, t-shirts, and other merchandise, as well as a detail of grim reaper-costumed security. Their outfits comprised the traditional black hoods and robes, and also intricately detailed skull masks and skeletal gloves.

While she didn't recognize all brand names present, Katherine knew enough of them to know that Jordan was most likely making a lot of money off of this event. *Huh. Maybe I've underestimated him.*

Kirk offered his arm. Katherine accepted it and they strolled up to the gate doors.

A grim reaper on the right got in their way. "Name?"

"Katherine Norrington, plus one."

Right Grim Reaper checked his phone. His head snapped back in what looked like either surprise or alarm. "*The* Katherine Norrington?"

Katherine looked at Kirk for confirmation. "As far as I know. Why?"

Right Grim Reaper didn't answer. He instead turned to his colleague. "Take Ms. Norrington's keys, valet her car nearby, maybe over there." He pointed to the left of the gate.

Left Grim Reaper nodded and held out his hand to accept Katherine's car keys. She took them out and deposited them.

"Which one?" Left Grim Reaper asked.

Katherine pointed to her car.

"Thanks, Ms. Norrington." Left Grim Reaper headed down the hill.

"If you'll follow me, Ms. Norrington?" Right Grim Reaper turned around and headed up the road to the mansion.

"*Ms.* Norrington?" Kirk wore a giant grin.

"Shut up," Katherine said.

"Fae and Mr. Blackstone are expecting you," Right Grim Reaper reported.

"Uh, expecting me for what?"

Right Grim Reaper turned around, but kept going. "Just expecting."

The coal-colored cobblestone road caught Katherine's eye. Someone had meticulously decorated the entire thing for the occasion. Rows of expertly carved jack-o'-lanterns lined both sides. Behind them stood mannequins representing the characters of various spooky folklore traditions. Vampires, ghosts, more grim reapers, mummies, even a few that Katherine didn't recognize, but which had all manner of black hoods, claws, or fangs.

About halfway up the hill, they could now hear Jordan's loud, thumping electronic dance music throb its way out of the entryway tower.

"Sounds like it's really happening," Kirk observed.

"What are you, Captain Seventies?" Katherine asked.

"No, Captain Twenties." He held up his toy Tommy gun.

Right Grim Reaper whipped out a walkie-talkie. The bony portion of his glove glowed brightly. He pressed the call button. "Security one to Fae. KN and plus one approaching. Over."

A young female voice answered. "Roger, security one. I will alert Fae. Over."

"Over and out." Right Grim Reaper put his walkie-talkie away.

"Wow, you're really dialed in—Or rather walkie-talkie'd in," Kirk said.

"Yeah. Weird," Katherine agreed.

Reaching the front doors, Right Grim Reaper opened them and stepped aside for Katherine and Kirk. His glowing skull mask looked very creepy floating in the shadows of the entryway tower and surrounding trees.

As they were about to enter, a tiny woman, Fae, with a very short, very fashionable haircut, dressed as some kind of nineteen twenties matron, came bursting out. "Katherine Norrington?"

"Um, yes?"

Fae rolled her eyes with relief. "Thank God! Jordan's been asking about you all night."

"Didn't it just start?"

"Not for Jordan." Fae led them inside.

As impressive as the gate and road up to the mansion had been, the hall was even more so. Multi-colored concert and disco-ball lights splashed all over the room. A DJ turntable stood at the top of the staircase, right below the plaque with the pendant's symbol. There, wearing a pair of giant headphones, Jordan mixed tracks.

On the ground floor, dozens of partygoers wore all kinds of costumes, from cheap, simple getups like the ones Katherine and Kirk had, to elaborate homemade ones. They danced, chatted, and engaged in several food and activity stations lining the wall. There was face painting, popcorn balls, a tub for apple bobbing, and on and on.

Katherine couldn't believe her eyes. Someone had cleaned the entire hall of all cobwebs and dust. In fact, even bigger, thicker fake ones had replaced the really dramatic ones that had once hung from Artemis and Apollo. *I seriously underestimated Jordan! Even the apple bobbing looks fun!*

Fae waved her hands all over Katherine's costume. "Love it. *Love* it!"

"Flapper." Katherine wasn't sure if Fae would have any idea.

"So now!" Fae declared, then turned her attention to Kirk. "And Tommy!"

"I think I'm supposed to be Al Capone or—" Kirk started.

Fae had long since lost interest in him. She held out her hand to Katherine. "Fae." She pointed to a sign Katherine hadn't yet noticed hanging on the wall to their right. It said F+E Events. "I'm the F."

"You said Fae?" Katherine was unsure she'd heard correctly over the booming music.

"Yep! As in Morgan le."

Katherine accepted Fae's hand. Fae shook firmly, then continued them on their way toward the staircase.

"Wow, pretty name," Kirk said.

Fae didn't bother looking at him. "Yep, I know. So"—she continued, only addressing Katherine—"Jordan's gonna want a quick check-in, then he'll wanna place you at the PoA."

"I'm sorry, check-in? PoA? 'Place'?"

Fae looked a little exasperated, as if she'd already explained this a billion times. She froze and faced both of them, though only kept her eyes on Katherine. "Check-in: check your pulse, see how you're feeling, feed you if necessary—Is that necessary? Have you eaten?"

Katherine opened her mouth to answer.

Fae continued her explanation. "Place: we're gonna station you at the hole above the grave in the west tower."

"Grave?" Katherine asked.

"Didn't you find some grave there?"

"I mean, it was more of a tomb, but yeah, I—"

"Tomb. Grave. That's the PoA, point of action, the place where it all went down, where you found the body."

*Not exactly* the *body, Fae. And why are you telling me as if you were the one who did it and I was only in the background?*

"Guests are gonna walk by, ask about it. We need you to narratively elaborate."

"You mean Kat's gonna stand there all night, wait for random people to happen to stop by, then tell them how she found the body?" Kirk asked.

Fae dropped her chin two full inches to accommodate the serious eye roll she now served him. "Um, that's what I *just* said."

"Wait. All night?" Katherine asked.

## THE POSSESSION OF BLACKSTONE MANSION

Fae stared at her as if she'd uttered an esoteric incantation from some obscure, dead language. "Yeah?"

*Goddamn it, Jordan!*

"Can she at least have company?" Kirk asked.

Fae sighed hard. Very hard. She pointed to Jordan's turntable. "Let's do your check-in." She resumed her march up.

Katherine and Kirk tried to keep up.

Passing by the statue of Artemis, Kirk gave it a quick, impressed nod. "Don't think I've ever seen it so"—he threw a glance up at all the dancing lights—"well lit."

Fae didn't pause or turn around. "Please do *not* touch the statues."

"I wasn't"—Kirk assured Katherine—"I wasn't gonna..."

Katherine patted his hand and whispered, "I know."

"JB! JB!" Fae shouted at Jordan.

Either deep into his mix or ignoring her, Jordan didn't look up.

"Jay! Bee!" Fae repeated.

Jordan finally deigned to lift his eyes to her, but then snapped his focus to Katherine and Kirk. "Kat!" His fingers danced across a few keys. The song continued. He tore off his headphones.

Seeming to well know her station in the hierarchy, Fae stepped far out of Jordan's way without another word as he left his turntable to greet Katherine.

"So glad you could make it!" Jordan exclaimed as he hugged Katherine.

"Didn't exactly leave me a choice!" Katherine said with a snarky smile.

Jordan leaned back and grinned at her dig. "Ahh!" He pointed both index fingers at her as if saying "You got me!"

Katherine returned the gesture, only with far more mockery of his.

"And who do we have here?" Jordan turned to Kirk.

"Jordan, Kirk. Kirk, Jordan," Katherine introduced.

Jordan took in both their costumes. "Love it. *Love* it! Roaring twenties!"

"The only kind!"

"You two good? Need something to eat? Something to drink? You got your pick of the food stations."

"Jordan?" Katherine pointed to her left.

"Oh? Problem? Issue? Need anything, you tell Fae," Jordan assured as he followed Katherine back down the staircase.

Katherine planted herself in front of Apollo. She crossed her arms. "Do I understand Fae correctly?"

# THE POSSESSION OF BLACKSTONE MANSION

"She's the best, isn't she? Totally pulled all this off in, like, twenty-four hours!" He looked over Katherine's shoulder, toward the front doors, then over Artemis's shoulders.

"You want me to hang out by the hole in the floor of the west tower and just kinda hope people drop by so I can tell them some sort of ghost story about Eileen?" Katherine asked.

Jordan kept looking about the room.

"What are you looking for?" she asked.

He froze as if she'd caught him doing something very naughty. "What? Nothing! Why?"

"Fine. Never mind," she said. "The west tower? I'm staying there? Like, all night?"

His jaw dropped, seemingly in protest, but then it closed. "I mean, that cool?"

"No, it's not cool! I thought you wanted me to attend this stupid thing just to, you know, lend some credibility or whatever."

"What's more credible than *the* antiques expert telling guests about *the* ultimate antique?"

"You're not seriously calling Eileen Byrne's desecrated remains an antique."

"Kat, you're the highlight of the whole thing!"

"I thought the mansion was the highlight of the whole thing."

"You're the highlight of the highlight!"

"All night?"

"Six hours."

"Jordan! I'm not standing around for six hours straight telling people about Eileen!"

"You'll get bathroom breaks."

She called up to the top of the staircase. "Kirk? We're outta here!"

Jordan jumped between her and Kirk. "Okay, I'm sorry, no, wait!" He chuckled as if he were embarrassed, but it sounded very rehearsed. "All night? Of course not. That's ridiculous. Who told you that?"

"Fae, then you confirmed."

"Fae, she gets stuff wrong all the time. I tell her paper cups, she gets Styrofoam."

"You said she was the best."

"At organizing!"

"Jordan, we're leaving."

"No, no, no, no, no. Fae'll get you a chair. I'll have her send over regular snacks, drinks, and stuff, tons of bathroom breaks. All the bathroom breaks in the world! Whatever you need. Seriously. Just please don't leave."

"I'll do it."

"Thank you!"

"For one hour."

His jaw dropped again.

"And if I wanna leave..." she trailed off.

# THE POSSESSION OF BLACKSTONE MANSION

He nodded very slowly. "Hey, if you gotta take off after one hour, even after food, drinks, and bathroom breaks, you know…"

She didn't budge.

"Would two hours be…?" he asked.

"You keep me fed and rested, and Kirk happy?"

Jordan looked around, seemingly already lost as to who this Kirk person was.

Katherine pointed behind him to poor Kirk waiting patiently at the top of the staircase. "He's right there! You just met him!"

"I know! I wanted to visually check on him." Jordan waved at Kirk.

Kirk waved back with a polite smile.

"As I was saying, I'm good and Kirk's happy, then yes, I think we can do two hours," Katherine said. "After that, though…"

"No, no, no," Jordan said. "After that, you kids gotta go to your monster mash or whatever, totally cool."

"Yes? Totally cool?"

He held up his palms in surrender. "Absolutely."

"Good."

"So, uh, when can we get you over there?"

She sighed and gave Kirk a thumbs up.

Fae leapt on that. She rushed past Kirk down the staircase, past Jordan, and laser focused on Katherine. "Follow me?"

"Don't you love them?" Jordan asked.

"Love!" Fae led Katherine and Kirk through the throng of partiers, down the hallway to the left of the staircase, to the west-east one, and finally to the west tower entrance.

## 24

The din of Jordan's music had all but disappeared in the dimly lit west-east hallway on the way to the west tower.

Katherine, Kirk, and Fae found a giant crowd before the west tower's entrance, eagerly awaiting Katherine's arrival.

"Oh my God," Katherine said, mostly to herself, but also to Kirk.

"Your devoted public."

"Right?" She counted at least twenty people all hanging around the tower's doors.

"Excuse us, everyone! Coming through!" Fae announced to the group.

Some people got out of the way, but most didn't seem to get the deeper meaning of Fae's words and stayed put.

Pushing past them, Fae stopped. She presented the tower doors to Katherine like an usher taking her to her seat.

Katherine opened the doors to find a similar, but much smaller setup, to the one in the entryway hall. There were lights standing on both sides of the room, with lots of lit candles circling the perimeter.

Starting from the room's symbol, printed pages of other similarly styled designs lined the wall in a vast circle going all the way to the doors. The display had the effect of adding spooky flare to the space while also obfuscating the original symbol.

*Is Jordan trying to hide the symbol?*

The organizers had set up a makeshift railing around the floor's hole. Katherine supposed Jordan had to do so for liability reasons, but it wasn't much of a barrier. If even one drunk reveler were to venture near... *Well, not my problem.*

"So if you could, uh..." Fae pointed to the space below the room's symbol.

"I'm over there?" Katherine asked.

"If you could." Fae offered a condescending grin.

Kirk moved to join her.

"What are you doing?" Fae asked.

"Keeping my girlfriend company."

Katherine's stomach fluttered. *Your girlfriend? Boy, are you getting laid tonight!*

"Um..." Fae's eyes darted between Katherine, Kirk, the awaiting mob, and farther down the hall. "Okay, um..."

"Promise I'll be quiet," Kirk offered.

"Ooh, okay." Fae seemed to work the arrangement over and over in her mind. "All right. Whatever. You're a plant."

"Behold my delicate branches." Kirk stretched his arms wide.

"Plants don't talk." Fae lowered his arms to his sides, then got out of his way.

Kirk walked over and stood proudly at Katherine's side.

"Girlfriend?" Katherine whispered.

Kirk grinned down at her.

"Listen up, everybody!" Fae said. "Ms. Norrington is ready to begin! The room has a legal capacity of twenty! If you are the twenty-first person, you are not coming in until that session has concluded. You will patiently wait your turn till the next session. If you have any issues, please do *not* bother Ms. Norrington. Please locate event staff and alert them. Are there any questions?"

Three people held up their hands, but she completely ignored them.

"Wonderful," Fae said. "First twenty. Have a happy Halloween!" She began her march back down the west-east hallway toward the entryway hall.

People filed in.

"So do you...?" Kirk asked Katherine.

"I don't know." She counted fifteen, sixteen. A twenty-first guy slid in. "Um, hey, man, I don't think you can..."

"Dude. Chick said only twenty," a man scolded Mr. Twenty-First.

"Seriously? Come on," Mr. Twenty-First whined.

"Only twenty, dude. Just wait," the man said.

Mr. Twenty-First groaned, exited, and slammed the door behind him.

"What a baby," a woman observed.

"Hey, everybody, so I'm Katherine Norrington."

Eighteen phones raised and started recording.

"I discovered the remains of Eileen Byrne." Katherine threw Kirk a look. *What am I supposed to do? Just step-by-step? I'm guessing Jordan wants it to be interesting. Arg. Why did I agree to this? Oh yeah, 'cause I had no friggin' choice!*

Kirk shook his head and shrugged.

*Screw it*, Katherine decided and forged ahead. "They'd buried her right down there." She pointed to the hole at their feet.

The crowd emitted at least fifteen "Ooh"s and a handful of "Whoa"s.

"She'd initially been buried in the grave of Silas Blackstone," Katherine continued, "but then they moved her here. Um, her fiancé attempted to murder her and then his brother finished her off."

"Always the fiancé," a woman said.

# THE POSSESSION OF BLACKSTONE MANSION

"Seriously. Or the husband," a second woman offered.

Katherine found she wasn't sure how to continue. She was no storyteller. At least not in this way. Thrust into a group of young people who were expecting a blood-soaked tale of murder and intrigue. "Turns out Eileen had been having an affair with her fiancé's father, Vernon Blackstone."

The crowd proclaimed another round of "Ooh"s.

"Oh my God, ew!" the first woman winced.

"Um, let me back up," Katherine said.

The guy who'd told Mr. Twenty-First to leave groaned. "Oh my God, this is terrible."

"Hey, let her finish," Kirk barked at him.

Katherine felt a nice tingle. *If these jerks weren't here, Kirk...* She surveyed the group's faces. Some were hanging on her every word. Some were still undecided. Some were long since checked out. "You guys wanna know what happened? What really happened? The seriously f'd-up version?"

Every face lit up.

"Buckle up, kiddies," Katherine warned, and plunged into every last gory detail of the vision Eileen had given her, without, of course, revealing how she'd acquired such knowledge.

Her strategy worked. She captivated every one of the group, even the guy who'd dared to groan.

*Maybe I'm not such a terrible storyteller!*

Right when she'd wrapped up the last detail of how Kirk and his crew had unearthed Eileen's remains, the doors opened and Fae stepped in.

"All right, people! Next session! Let's go!" Fae practically yanked the group out of the room.

The crowd got what was going on and filed out.

"Uh, Fae?" Katherine asked.

"Next session, next session, let's go!" Fae didn't seem to have heard Katherine.

"Fae, I'm gonna..." Katherine pointed out the door.

Fae looked both confused and deeply offended. "That was only the first session."

"Jordan promised regular bathroom breaks."

"You need a bathroom break?"

"Yes."

"After only one session?"

"Yes."

"You're kidding me."

"Will you get outta the way, Fae?" Kirk asked.

Fae held up a finger. "Wow, dude. Could not *wait* to inject your phallocentric, patrio-hierarchical bullshit."

"Patrio-hierarchical...?"

"Fae?" Katherine asked.

Fae now gave her the eye roll she'd previously only given Kirk. She stepped out of the way and held the door open.

Katherine grabbed Kirk's hand and walked out. Making it only a few feet down the hallway, she looked back at Fae. "Where are they?"

"What?" Fae now didn't even try to conceal her irritation.

"The bathrooms?"

"Out the front, around the corner."

"In front of the house? Outside?" Kirk asked.

"Yes," Fae drew out the "s" as if she'd explained this, too, a billion times.

"Come on." Katherine smiled at Kirk and led him to the entryway.

Stepping into the giant thumping space, Katherine drew Kirk closer. "So let's go outside just for a quick breather, come back in, get something to drink or whatever. Then, if you see Fae, let me know, and we'll disappear again."

"*Love* it!" Kirk laughed, mocking Jordan's and Fae's earlier expression.

Katherine led him first to the perimeter of the room, hoping they could avoid the throbbing crowd, but found the space around the food and activity stations impossible to navigate. She then dragged him through the middle of the dancing crowd.

It was an adventure weaving past drunk revelers who paid zero attention to the two people attempting to move past them. Katherine kept a firm grasp on Kirk's hand.

Then she lost it. She turned around to find him four people back. He was catching up, but...

She felt like she was being watched. With so many people in here, such a notion was hardly surprising, but she couldn't shake it. She searched the crowd. Dancing twentysomething after dancing twentysomething.

*Wait.* She looked back at a space she'd already searched. There, behind the rest of the crowd, up against the wall, stood the man in black. "Kirk!"

Kirk joined her. "Yeah?"

"Do you see that guy over there?" She pointed.

He shook his head. "What guy?"

"Black hat, black glasses..." She looked back to where she'd seen the man, but he was gone. She scanned the crowd surrounding the area where she thought she'd seen him.

He'd vanished.

"Maybe we should..." She scanned the area between where they were standing and the front doors. There was a churros station. "Wanna get some churros?"

"Sure, I guess," Kirk said.

She took his hand and led them to the station. "Hey, can we get two orders?" she asked the guy manning the station.

"What do you want on them?" the guy asked.

"Uh, I dunno. Cinnamon? Chocolate?"

The lights went out. It was completely black.

Some of the crowd screamed. Some cheered.

Katherine spun around. She saw Kirk nowhere. "Kirk?"

"Kat! I'm right here!" he shouted over the din.

She didn't see him and as he spoke, he sounded like he was getting farther and farther away.

She attempted to orient herself, but it was impossible. She had no idea whether she was still facing the churros station, the wall, or the staircase. She dug out her phone and turned on its flashlight.

Excited, shifting bodies filled her vision. There was not one sign of Kirk's pinstripe suit or his beautiful eyes. *Don't panic, don't panic*, she repeated to herself as panic surged inside her. *Okay, find a wall. Any wall.* She pushed forward, shoving limbs and torsos aside. She struggled against the mounting headache arising from all the screams.

Flat. She pressed her hands against it. A wall. *All I gotta do is follow it.* She inched her way along to her right. That direction seemed as good as any.

She felt the deepest, coldest chill stab straight into her chest and cut down her spine. She didn't know how she knew, but she knew. *They're here.*

She turned around. She saw nothing but the crowd. Pushing, shoving, anonymous throngs.

*There.* On the other side of the room, near the left of the staircase, she saw a woman. She had a pale glow about her. It was enough that Katherine could see her, but not so much that it looked like it had any actual source. The woman was deathly pale. Her eyes had sunken into their sockets. Her lips had receded from her teeth. Her hair was still up in a fancy bun. Her arms were thinner than her pictures, but her torso was more bloated. *Gloria.*

Gloria drifted through the crowd slowly, but with the determination of a woman who knew exactly what she wanted.

Straight for Katherine.

But Gloria wasn't the only one. Katherine could feel that others were here. She searched the darkness and not far to Gloria's right saw a man she knew instantly. *Vernon.*

Finally, Katherine looked to Vernon's right and soon located another man, shorter and slighter than Vernon. He bore the telltale hole in the upper left of his chest. *Reginald.*

Katherine stepped back, but she knew the movement was futile. These spirits intended to commune with her and commune they would. "All right, come on! What are you waiting for?"

The very next moment, Gloria, Vernon, and Reginald were right in front of her. In her personal

# THE POSSESSION OF BLACKSTONE MANSION

space. They seized her hand that was holding up her phone.

The last thing Katherine saw was the device drop from her fingers, its light dying in an impossibly deep black abyss.

## 25

Katherine was floating in a black void. Her arms thrust forward and her legs kicked, but she felt no wetness. It was cold all around her, but it didn't bother her. All these sensations were so familiar. She'd already gone to this place, taken this journey with Eileen Byrne weeks ago.

*Who's showing me what now?*

When she'd been with Eileen, she'd seen everything the night of Eileen's murder quite literally from Eileen's perspective. If there was anything beyond Eileen's field of vision, Katherine didn't see it.

A pinpoint of light appeared. *Here we go.* The light grew and grew until it had become a horizontal cone. Inside the base of the cone, she could see the vague, blurry shapes of two people standing close together. The one on the left looked like it might be a young woman. She was at least a foot shorter than the one on the right.

As the background came into focus, Katherine recognized it as a room in Blackstone mansion,

# THE POSSESSION OF BLACKSTONE MANSION

though she didn't know which one. Its wallpaper and furniture, though, were unmistakable.

Now the one light cone had separated into two. What she was seeing was the point of view of someone unseen looking in on two other people through the crack of an open door. *They're spying on them!*

The scene before her was finally clear. Someone was watching Eileen speaking in hushed tones to Vernon. Katherine still couldn't quite hear what they were saying, so she floated into the room and listened.

"There's nothing to worry about," Eileen said. "I've located it already. All we have to do..."

"I don't know, darling," Vernon said. "I just don't know."

"I thought you loved me."

"I do! I do. Of course I do. But I don't know if I can... Gloria, we've been married so long."

"You said you hadn't felt passion for her in years!"

"It's not so straight-forward, Eileen. We have the two boys, the estate, the company."

"You told me you wanted to be with me! That she'd never grant you a divorce!"

"She never would."

"Then this is the only way. You said yourself that she's never been happy. Why not end her suffering? Like you would a wounded doe?"

*Damn, Eileen. Cold.*

"I have a solution," Vernon said. "No one has to die. I don't have to try to get Gloria to grant me a divorce."

"I don't understand," Eileen said. "What would we do?"

"Marry my son. Marry Reginald."

"But he hasn't even asked me."

"He will."

"I don't know, Vern."

He put his hands on her shoulders. "It will work perfectly. You'll be in the family, legally. We can be together when Reggie isn't around, and, well, he can handle your bakery."

"But he'll want to"—she lowered her voice even more—"consummate."

Vernon sighed. "Yes, I'm afraid that can't be helped, but there are things you can do."

"Like what?"

"Feign a headache. Pretend he's me. Someone else."

"No, I couldn't possibly. I..."

He struggled to keep his voice down. "I do it all the time with Gloria!"

Katherine heard a very irritated grunt from the gap between the door and its frame. *Yeah, I wouldn't be too pleased to hear that either.*

"What was that?" Eileen asked.

"Mother?" a muffled, but very familiar, voice uttered.

The sight line swung to the left, away from the door. It landed on Marcus, who stood a few feet away. "Quiet!" Gloria whispered harshly as she marched right over to him.

*So this is Gloria's vision? Doesn't exactly look like she's in mortal danger.*

"What on earth are you doing?" Marcus asked. "Why, are you eavesdropping? On father?"

"Don't you have a horse to ride or a butler to chastise?" Gloria demanded.

---

Katherine felt a sudden shift, as if she were on a boat about to capsize. The next thing she knew, Gloria's vision had vanished, and she was now seeing a new light pinpoint. When this scene came into focus, it was outside. The woods. A beautiful, cloudless day. The owner of the vision was hiking on uneven ground. Two hands gripped a rifle that swung back and forth as the person walked.

"I say, Marcus, I don't even believe it's pheasant season," Reginald said.

*So am I with Reginald now?*

"I may have been mistaken." There was a distance in Marcus's voice. Deep distraction.

Reginald's field of vision turned around to face Marcus, who was holding his own rifle, though much more tightly, his knuckles solid white.

The mansion loomed in the background, its onyx walls a brutal contrast against the blue sky. For the first time since Katherine had ever seen the house, the twilight that always seemed to linger over it wasn't present.

"I say, old boy, you all right? You look..." Reginald said.

Marcus paused. "How do I look?"

"It's nothing, Marcus. It's just you look a little..." Reginald walked the few steps to his brother. He lightly embraced him. Marcus looked disgusted at the gesture. "It's mother, isn't it? You're still missing her?"

Marcus sighed with relief. "Yes. That... That must be it."

"Well, come on. Let's get us some dinner," Reginald suggested. He then resumed his hike down the hill.

A still few seconds followed. Katherine heard only the distant song of birds and the nearby crunch of boots on grass.

*Blam!* A gunshot rang out.

Reginald gasped as he froze. His rifle dropped. He sank to his knees. He looked down. Blood trickled out from a huge hole in the upper left of his chest.

Feet ran up behind him. He looked up. Marcus peered down at him, his eyes crawling all over him.

"Mar..." Reginald attempted to speak.

Marcus put a finger to his lips. "Shh... Sh, sh, sh, sh... Won't be long now."

Reginald fell to his right side, then onto his back. "Mar... Why...?"

Marcus stood over him. "Yes, that should do nicely. If my anatomy is correct, you have approximately three minutes at the most."

Reginald tried to say something else, but all that came out was wheezing gurgles.

"Try not to talk, Reggie. That will only exacerbate it." Marcus walked around behind his brother, took his arms, and dragged him back toward the mansion. He sounded extremely enthralled as he explained everything. "You see, your left lung is filling with blood. Therefore, any attempt to speak will only apply pressure, thereby accelerating the... your death."

Reginald wheezed some more.

"Not to worry, Reggie," Marcus said. "I'll have you back in the house in one minute."

He must have been dragging his brother as hard as he could because in only a few more seconds, Reginald saw the top of the mansion's open front door frame, followed by the entryway hall's ceiling.

"Master Marcus, what happened?" a butler asked.

"Reginald has been accidentally shot." Marcus kept his eyes on Reginald, possibly waiting for the specific moment of death.

"Are *you* all right, Master Marcus?"

"Don't worry about me! Get some pillows or bedding or whatever! I want my brother to be as comfortable as possible!"

"Shouldn't we call the doctor?"

"Are you daft? There's no time for that! Pillows now!"

"Right away, Master Marcus."

Katherine heard feet run away as fast as they could.

Marcus's face turned in Reginald's field of vision until it was right side up.

Katherine couldn't tell, but it looked like the tiniest, most microscopic bit of sadness might be washing over Marcus's expression. *You little shit.*

"The... money...?" Reginald asked.

Marcus's face lit up. He laughed out loud. "The money? *Your* money? Oh, honestly, Reggie, you really are quite stupid. No, this wasn't about our respective portions of the inheritance." He looked up, contemplating that. "I mean, yes, it will be nice to get all of it now, but no." He looked back down at his brother and grinned wider than Katherine had ever seen. "No, no. This wasn't about that."

"Wh...?"

"I suppose it no longer matters given that you have, what, twenty more seconds?" Marcus leaned down, past Reginald's sight line, to his ear, and whispered. "I found them, Reg. Great-grandfather Silas's notes. And oh, the wonderful things they divulged. There's a place. He called it the Realm."

*Realm? That's what Nigel said!*

"He was obsessed with it. Absolutely obsessed. It drove him mad. You see, there's a Formula, and with it I'll be able to—" Marcus's monologue ceased.

---

That capsizing-boat sensation hit again. Reginald's vision vanished. Katherine swam in the void. A new light pinpoint soon appeared. The resulting vision was very familiar. The Blackstones' dining room. The only actual difference between this vision and Eileen's was that this was from Gloria's point of view onto the rest of her family. Vernon sat opposite her, at the other end of the table. Marcus was at her right. Reginald her left, his head drooping slightly. They were in the middle of a soup course.

"Honestly, mother, if you don't like it, we can always fire the chef," Marcus said.

"Fire Gregoire? But his pastries are brilliant!" Vernon slurped his soup with the echoing volume of a two-year-old who hadn't yet mastered spoons.

"Brilliant, but not the best," Reginald said quietly. He stirred his spoon round and round in his bowl.

Marcus chuckled. "Reg, are you still stuck on that..."—he snapped his fingers, trying to remember—"Blast. What was her name? Dorothy? Blanche? Gertrude?"

Reginald hammered his fists on the table. His spoon bounced right out of his bowl. "Eileen!"

The rest of the family fell silent.

*Huh. Guess ol' Reg still feels bad about murdering his girlfriend.*

"I don't care what you all say, this tastes funny." Gloria scooped up another spoonful of soup.

Marcus watched with eager eyes as she sipped.

Vernon sighed. "Marcus is right, Reginald. It's high time to move on. Plenty more fish in the sea. Why I was just talking to George the other day. Do you know he has a lovely young niece right about your age?"

Reginald stood up. "I'm not hungry."

"Oh come, Reg," Marcus said. "I'm sorry. There. Better?"

Gloria coughed.

"What's that, dear?" Vernon asked.

"I didn't say anything, Vernon." Gloria coughed again. "I coughed." And again and again.

"What's wrong, mother?" A grin rose on Marcus's lips. "Down the wrong pipe?"

Reginald stayed standing, his eyes focused on Gloria. "Mother?"

"Not down the wrong"—Gloria coughed three times in quick succession—"bloody pipe!" She tried to stand, but tripped backward over her chair and fell to the floor. Her coughing continued.

"Mother!" Reginald cried and ran to her side.

"Dear, are you all right?" Vernon stood.

Marcus neither said nor asked anything. He stood up from the table and knelt next to her.

She saw all three men's faces gazing down. Reginald looked concerned, Vernon baffled, and Marcus delighted, though he was trying very hard to hide it.

"Call... the... doctor... you... useless..." Gloria demanded.

"The doctor! Of course!" Vernon jumped up and ran out of her field of vision.

"I'll get some sheets, a pillow." Reginald also stood and ran.

With the other two gone, Marcus leaned over her, closing in on her face. "That's it, mother. It will all be over soon."

"Mar... cus... you... bastard... Why?" Gloria's vision already clouded with black spots.

Marcus leaned in even closer, till his face took up all of Gloria's view. He whispered. "I had to cull the strongest first, mother. You understand. Say hello to Silas. And Eileen." He smiled wide.

"Bas... tard...!" Gloria sputtered before further coughing overtook her throat.

Vernon and Reginald returned. Reginald clumsily shoved a pillow under Gloria's head.

"The doctor's on his way, Gloria," Vernon reported.

The black spots now took up more space than anything else in Gloria's view.

"Gloria? Gloria!" Vernon said.

Gloria's vision dissolved to black.

*You little bastard.*

---

The capsize hit. Another light pinpoint appeared. This new vision also revealed a very familiar space. Recently familiar. It was the tomb in which Katherine found Vernon's corpse. It was aglow with a flickering light. The point of view was from someone running, stumbling, and tripping up the tomb's spiral staircase toward its exit. The someone was struggling not only to move, but to maintain his hold on his torch.

"Marcus, wait!" Vernon shouted. He saw a glint of Marcus's smirking face just beyond the point at which the staircase reached the ground floor, outside of where the rising stone step could seal Vernon in.

Even in the faint light, Vernon could clearly see the reflecting platinum of the pendant dangling from Marcus's neck.

"I'm sorry, father, but I simply have no further use for you," Marcus said with mocking lament.

"Marcus, it doesn't have to be this way!" Vernon cried. "I forgive you for your brother and mother! I forgive you for Eileen! Please!"

But it was far too late. Marcus disappeared from view and one second later, that fatal stone step began its rise from the floor to the top of the staircase's tunnel. In mere moments, Vernon would be trapped.

He reached the raised stone wall the second it had finished its ascent. "Please! Please." He breathed slowly to calm himself down, most likely already accepting his fate. He stared into the torch's playful flame. "We can forget all about them. We can leave this damned, detestable mountain. I'll sell the company. Sell the mansion. Sell everything. We'll escape to Europe. Wander her streets. Her plazas."

Katherine could hear him weep.

"I'm so sorry, Gloria," Vernon said. "I'm so sorry. I... I did the best I could. I loved those boys. But... but Reginald was always so very weak. And Marcus so... What could I have done?"

*Man, almost feel sorry for the old guy.*

"I suppose once you go out, that will be about that," Vernon referred to the torch's flame. He sat up against the wall and chuckled. "That will be that."

His eyes stayed on the flame till it weakened and faded. As it was about to wink away, he saw the tiniest movement in the distance. A shadow within the shadows. It slithered along the wall toward him. It had a vaguely human shape. He shuddered at the accompanying chill. "Gloria?"

The shadow ceased its movement inches from his face. It made no attempt to reach out to him. It seemed only to sit there and gaze.

"Oh my dearest Gloria."

As its last little embers died, the torch fell into his lap, where it let out a tiny *hiss*.

Then nothing but silent black.

## 26

Light flooded Katherine's world. Then came the voices. Excited chattering voices. She heard a loud gasp. *Is that me?* She hardly had time to consider who'd let it out when her blurred vision swung over to the right and she heard someone upchuck hard.

Her vision cleared enough to see a small pool of vomit directly in front of her on a surface of dull metal.

"That's it. You're okay," Kirk said.

Katherine fell back to lying down. Kirk was above her, in front of a bright lamp. On her sides, there were three uniformed medical personnel. Kirk wiped her mouth with a cloth.

"Where... Where am I?" she asked.

"Ambulance. You're fine," he said. "You passed out soon after the lights went out."

*The lights. Oh my God, that's right! The mansion! Jordan's stupid party! The man! The man in black! Who was he? And the Blackstones. They all...* "Marcus. Kirk, it was Marcus."

"Don't worry about that right now. Let's just get you to a hospital."

"No." She sat up.

He gently pressed her back down. "Kat, please. You were out, like, unresponsive, for, like, ten minutes."

"It was Marcus, Kirk. It was Marcus all along. It wasn't just Eileen he murdered. He killed his whole damn family."

"Shh. It's okay. Right now, just relax."

"He planned it. The whole thing. That's why Gloria and Reginald died exactly a year apart. He probably had to make it seem like it was random. And he was so goddamn wealthy, no authorities were gonna question him."

"Kat? Please, breathe."

"He got away with it. He got away with all of it! The little shit!"

Kirk didn't respond. He scooped up her hand and clenched it tight.

"I gotta... I gotta talk to Jordan. Or maybe not. I gotta figure out why. Why did Marcus kill them all? He said the Formula and Realm."

She finally took Kirk's advice and tried to relax. It didn't go so well as all these thoughts fought each other for space in her mind. "Silas's notes. It all goes back to Silas. The Formula. The Realm. Silas."

Her world fell dark again.

---

K atherine woke up in a hospital bed.
"Hey, there you are," Kirk said.

She found him sitting to her left. To her right, there sat a giant bouquet, its wrapping paper concealing the flowers within. Behind it closed curtains let only a few rays of morning daylight trickle in. "Hey. How long've I been out?"

"Just the rest of the night."

"Have you been here the whole time?"

He nodded.

She giggled. "You must be exhausted."

"Don't worry about that."

"Wow, what happened?"

"You passed out, stayed out, we got you into that ambulance, you came to, passed out again."

She nodded. "Yeah."

"Think it was something you ate? If so, you could probably squeeze a bit outta Jordan."

She shook her head. "No. It was somebody I met."

"Sorry?"

"How long do I have to be in here?"

"Not sure. I think they wanna keep you here at least a day or two for observation."

"Fine, but after that—"

"Kat, I think you need to take some time off."

"What do you mean?"

"You've been going and going, well, since you arrived here."

"Well, stuff's been going down."

"I think you need to not worry about all that stuff."

"Are you kidding me? I found Eileen."

"I know."

"And you were there when I found the others."

He nodded.

"All of whom Marcus murdered," she said.

"And he's been dead for how long?"

"Doesn't matter."

"I think it does."

"Why?"

"Because look where you are. You need to chill."

"Don't—" She caught herself before she raised her voice. "I need to understand what happened. Why Marcus did it. Why those crazy tombs are sitting under that mansion. Why its whole friggin' floor plan is the same as an occult symbol that guy Nigel was terrified of."

Kirk's face fell. "Well, right now, you need to be under observation."

"Fine. Guess I can't do anything from here, anyway."

"That's right."

"What's this?" She pointed to the bouquet.

"Dunno."

"You didn't bring 'em?"

"Wish I had."

She grinned. "You could've taken credit."

"I dunno about that. They're huge, but pretty weird."

"What do you mean?"

He stood, walked over to the bouquet, and turned it so she could see its contents.

Black roses. Dozens of them. It was at once the most tortured-looking and beautiful thing she'd ever seen. Someone had arranged the roses quite delicately with greens. A card with her name written in exquisite calligraphy lay in the middle. The whole arrangement was very professional and, she guessed, very expensive.

She sighed hard. "Luke."

"Guess he still hasn't gotten the message," Kirk said.

"What in the hell?" she asked the bouquet, then glanced at him. "Hand me my phone?"

"You sure that's a good idea?"

She nodded. He gave her the phone. She angrily tapped in Luke's number.

Luke answered immediately. "Hey, Kat, what's goin' on?"

"Oh, you're hilarious," she said.

"Sorry?"

"Luke, I thought I was clear."

"About...?"

"Us!"

"You were."

"Where are you, like, in some swanky Portland presidential suite?"

"No. I'm back home. New York."

"Then what, you had them ordered ahead of time? How'd you even know I'm in the hospital?"

"Kat, I don't know—You're in the hospital?"

"The roses, Luke! The frickin' *black* roses? I mean, come on. What is this? You're, like, officially burying our relationship? What are you, six?"

"Katherine, I swear, I don't know what you're talking about."

"Gimme a break. First you showed up at my apartment, then the first bouquet, then at my work. You honestly expect me to believe you didn't send me another bouquet?"

"Yes, I expect you to believe that because I didn't."

She yanked the card from its little stand and tore it open. "Oh, this is rich. A friggin' poem? 'Dean and Kat drove o'er the bridge Since he and Ryan had fought—' That's great, Luke. Really nice."

Luke took a very deep breath. "Katherine, I need you to listen to me. I never sent flowers. I never sent a note. And I certainly wouldn't have, after all we've fought about and talked about, been so insensitive as to include a cheeseball poem about you and Dean."

She paused. A chill almost as intense as the ones she'd felt around the spirits ran down her spine. She checked the card, the envelope, the sides of the bouquet, and its bottom. "There's no return address. No vendor."

"I dunno what to tell you, but I swear I didn't send them."

She eyed Kirk. He shrugged.

"It's okay, Luke," she said. "I believe you."

"You okay, Kat? You sound..." Luke trailed off.

"I'm fine. I apologize for having bothered you."

"No, it's okay. I just wanna make sure you're—"

She hung up. She knew she was being rude to him, but at this moment, that was the least of her concerns. She looked over the poem again.

> *Dean and Kat drove o'er the bridge*
> *Since he and Ryan had fought*
> *Dean fell in, Kat didn't reach him*
> *So he died there on the spot*

She almost admired it. Someone had crafted it well. A near-perfect conversion of *Jack and Jill* for that terrible night when she'd lost Dean.

That terrible night. It had haunted her ever since. Not just because of Dean's death, but because of everything that had followed. The fallout with

Dean's widower Ryan, with their and Katherine's mutual friends, and with her and Dean's family. The need for her to get away as far as she could. Which led to her arrival in Blackstone and the mansion and Eileen and all of it.

Had Katherine not driven with Dean that terrible night, would she be here right now? "They know."

"Who knows?" Kirk asked.

"They know everything about me they needed to know to get under my skin. The worst thing about me. The most painful." Whoever wrote these lines knew she'd blamed herself for Dean's death.

She read the second line over again. "'Since he and Ryan had fought...'" That was two intimate details the author knew. What had led to the accident, which she hadn't told the police, and how she felt about it afterwards. *Didn't reach him.* Not "couldn't." Didn't.

She leaned back against the wall and let her hands holding the card fall to her lap. She thought about the last weeks since she'd arrived in Blackstone. What could have triggered this. It wasn't her involvement in the affairs of Blackstone mansion. Otherwise, this kind of thing would have happened after her first contact with Jordan. It wasn't after her contact with the police after they'd found Eileen's remains. *Nigel.* It was after she'd reached out to Miles

# THE POSSESSION OF BLACKSTONE MANSION

and his friend Nigel regarding the symbol on the pendant.

She picked up her phone.

"Who you calling now?" Kirk asked.

She didn't answer him. She located Nigel's number in her outgoing call list and tapped the call icon. The line rang.

"Hello?" Nigel asked.

"Hi, Nigel."

"Yes. Who's this?" His tone already sounded exceedingly suspicious.

"It's Kat. Um, Katherine Norrington? Miles's friend?"

It sounded like it took Nigel two hard seconds to remember who the hell she was. "Ah, yes. Hello, Kat. I'd thought our business had concluded."

"Yes, you'd answered my questions."

"Then, Kat, I don't mean to be insufferably rude, but what are we doing on the phone?"

"Nigel, did you have flowers sent to me?"

"I'm sorry?" His tone sounded beyond incredulous, like such a notion seemed impossible to even contemplate.

"Did you order a bouquet of"—*black*—"roses to be sent to my hospital room?"

"At the expense of repeating myself, Kat, I truly don't mean to be rude, but what the hell are you talking about?"

*It wasn't him.* She could hear it in his voice. He really had no idea. She was intensely relieved, especially because the very act of talking to someone as eccentric as Nigel was immensely taxing. But now she was back to square one. *If not him, who?* "I'm sorry, Nigel. It's nothing. Crazy-sounding. You'd only... Never mind."

"Very well. Good night... or day."

"Wait. Please."

"Yes?"

*You have him on the phone. Might as well squeeze out of him what you can.* "The symbol that Miles sent you."

"Yes?" His tone now sounded like the only other thing he wanted to hear from her was "goodbye."

"Did you show it to anyone else?"

"Well, I suppose that depends on what you mean by 'anyone else.'"

*Now what the hell are* you *talking about? You either showed it to someone else or you didn't!* "What do *you* mean by 'anyone else'?"

"Did I sit down with someone at coffee and pass them a full-color printout on glossy paper?"

"Yeah?"

"No. I did not."

"Then what do you mean?"

"I posted the picture on several fora specializing in this sort of thing. A bit of a crowd source, if you will."

# THE POSSESSION OF BLACKSTONE MANSION

*Wonderful. He pasted it all over the goddamn internet. That means anyone anywhere could've seen it, could've made plans, could've... Fantastic.* "I thought you were an expert." Her tone sounded much more harshly accusatory than she'd intended.

"I am," he said plainly. "But hive mind and all that."

"I see."

"Was there anything else, Kat?"

"No. Thank you for your time, Nigel."

"You're quite welcome, Kat. Good afternoon or morning or whatever." He hung up.

She stared into space, holding her phone out as if she still needed quick access to it.

She felt the device lift from her fingers. Kirk was setting it aside.

"Kirk?" she asked.

"Yeah?"

"Can you stay with me? Just till I pass out?"

"I'm not going anywhere."

As she drifted off, she couldn't help but run over everything in her head. *Why'd he kill them all? Why build those tombs? What is up with that symbol?* She had no idea, but she was going to find out.

---

The story concludes in book three,
*THE FALL OF BLACKSTONE MANSION!*

## AUGUSTINE PIERCE

Start reading now!

# The Fall of Blackstone Mansion
# The Blackstone Trilogy Book 3

Katherine can't escape the pull of the haunted Blackstone mansion, even though it has already threatened her sanity—and her life.

Desperate to uncover its secrets, she digs deeper into the mysteries of the Blackstone family, only to find herself entangled in a web of supernatural intrigue that spans generations. As she peels back layers of dark history, Katherine realizes the mansion's ghosts are more than just restless spirits—they're harbingers of a terrible truth that could consume her.

With each revelation, the line between the living and the dead blurs, and Katherine must confront the possibility that she's in over her head. The shadows of Blackstone mansion hide more than just family skeletons; they conceal a power that could reshape reality itself.

As the boundary between worlds crumbles, Katherine faces an impossible choice: walk away and preserve her sanity, or risk everything to uncover the mansion's ultimate secret—and possibly join the very entities that haunt its halls.

In this heart-pounding supernatural thriller, Katherine must decide if satisfying her curiosity is worth the price of her soul. Because in Blackstone mansion, some secrets are better left buried.

***Start reading the terrifying conclusion
to the Blackstone trilogy now!***

Get your free book, *Zoe's Haunt*, by joining Augustine Pierce's newsletter. You can unsubscribe at any time.

# Acknowledgments

Thanks to my cover designers at MiblArt, who created a fantastic cover.

# DARK REALM

The Blackstone Trilogy

*The Haunting of Blackstone Mansion*
*The Possession of Blackstone Mansion*
*The Fall of Blackstone Mansion*

## Also by Augustine Pierce

*The Curse of Braddock Mansion*

Horror in Paradise

*Cenote*

*Arena*

*Down*

## About the Author

Augustine Pierce is the author of *The Curse of Braddock Mansion, Cenote, Zoe's Haunt, Arena, Down, The Haunting of Blackstone Mansion, The Possession of Blackstone Mansion,* and *The Fall of Blackstone Mansion*. He lives in Paris with his wife and collection of horror board games. He enjoys travel, snorkeling, and all things macabre.

Stay in touch! Subscribe to Augustine Pierce's newsletter and follow his Facebook page!

authoraugustinepierce@gmail.com

Printed in Great Britain
by Amazon